Praise for *New York Times* bestselling author
Lynsay Sands and the Argeneau series

LOVE BITES

'Readers will be highly amused, very satisfied, and eager
for the next Argeneau tale'
Booklist

'With its whip-smart dialogue and sassy characters,
Love Bites . . . is a great romantic comedy worth tasting'
Romance Reviews Today

SINGLE WHITE VAMPIRE

'A cheeky, madcap tale . . . vampire lovers will find
themselves laughing throughout'
Publishers Weekly

'*Single White Vampire* is a wonderfully funny, fast-moving
story that's an absolute delight to read . . . Fans of humorous
romance won't want to miss this one, even if vampires aren't
their cup of tea'
Romantic Times BOOKreviews

TALL, DARK & HUNGRY

'Delightful and full of interesting characters and romance'
Romantic Times BOOKreviews

'*Tall, Dark & Hungry* takes us on an heartwarming journey of
healing hearts and sizzling attraction as Bastien and Terri race
through New York and around the world in search of love'
A Romance Review

The Argeneau Vampire series by Lynsay Sands:

Love Bites

Single White Vampire

Tall, Dark & Hungry

A Quick Bite

A Bite to Remember

Bite Me if you Can

The Accidental Vampire

Vampires Are Forever

Vampire Interrupted

The Rogue Hunter

The Immortal Hunter

The Renegade Hunter

Single White Vampire

LYNSAY SANDS

First published in Great Britain in 2010 by
Gollancz
An imprint of the Orion Publishing Group
Orion House, 5 Upper St Martin's Lane, London WC2H 9EA
An Hachette UK Company

3 5 7 9 10 8 6 4 2

A CIP catalogue record for this book is available
from the British Library

ISBN 978 0 575 09383 6

Typeset by carrstudio.co.uk

Printed in Great Britain by
Clays Ltd, St Ives plc

www.lynsaysands.net

www.orionbooks.co.uk

The Orion Publishing Group's policy is to use papers that are
natural, renewable and recyclable products and made from wood
grown in sustainable forests. The logging and manufacturing
processes are expected to conform to the environmental regulations
of the country of origin.

Single White Vampire

To Bobby, Shirley and Reg, Cathy and Bill, Mo, Darryl, and David. For the friendship and the love. Thanks for adopting me.

Prologue

January 30th

Dear Mr. Argeneau:

    I hope this letter gets to you, finds you well, and that you had a happy holiday season. This is the second communication I've sent. The first was mailed just before Christmas. No doubt it was lost in the holiday confusion. I did attempt to contact you by telephone; unfortunately, the contact information we have doesn't include your phone number, and it is apparently unlisted.

    As to the reason for writing; I am pleased to inform you that the vampire series you write under the name Luke Amirault is quite popular with readers—much more so than we ever expected. There has even been a great deal of interest in a possible book-signing tour. So many stores have contacted us regarding this possibility that I thought I should contact you and find out if and when you would be interested in undertaking such an endeavor.

1

Please contact this office with your phone number and your response.

I look forward to hearing from you.

Sincerely,

Kate C. Leever

Editor

Roundhouse Publishing Co., Inc.

New York, NY

April 1st

Dear Ms. Leever:

No.

Sincerely,

Lucern Argeneau

Toronto, Ontario

April 11th

Dear Mr. Argeneau:

I received your letter this morning and, while I gather you are not interested in a book-signing tour, I feel I should stress just how strong is the public's interest in your books. Your popularity is growing rapidly. Several publications have written requesting an interview. I don't think I need explain how helpful such publicity would be to future sales.

As to a book-signing tour, not only have we had phone calls regarding one, but a highly successful bookstore chain with outlets in both Canada and the United States has announced that it would be willing to foot the bill to have you visit their larger stores. They would arrange and pay for your flights, put you up in hotels at each stop, and supply a car and driver to collect you from the airport, see you to the hotel, then to the signing and back. This is no small offer, and I urge you to consider it carefully.

As mail from here to Toronto appears to be quite slow—though your return letters seem to take the usual ten days—I am sending this by overnight express. I would appreciate your immediate response—and please remember to include your phone number this time.

Sincerely,
Kate C. Leever
Editor
Roundhouse Publishing Co., Inc.
New York, NY

June 15th
Dear Ms. Leever:
    No.
Sincerely,
Lucern Argeneau
Toronto, Ontario

June 26th
Dear Mr. Argeneau:
    Once again you have forgotten to include your phone number. That being the case, I would first ask that you please call the office at once and speak to either myself, or, if I should happen to be unavailable when you call, my assistant Ashley. You may call collect if necessary, but I would really like to talk to you myself because I feel sure that you may not realize how popular you have become, or how important and necessary contact with your readers can be.

I do not know if you're aware of it, but fan sites are springing up all over the Internet and we receive tons of mail daily for you which will be boxed and forwarded to you separate from this letter. I have mentioned the requests for a book-signing tour in previous letters, but should tell you that those requests are now reaching unmanageable proportions. It seems almost every bookstore around the world would love to have you visit and are sure the signing would be a major success. While you could not possibly hit every store, we think that one store in every major city would be manageable.

I would also like to urge you to consider giving an interview or two, and am including the letters we have received from various publications regarding this. As you will notice, these requests come from more than just romance publications. Your popularity has gone mainstream, as is reflected by the fact that various newspapers and literary magazines are also requesting interviews. We have even had interest from a couple of the morning news shows. While the news shows would have to be in person, the newspaper and magazine interviews need not be; they could be managed either over the phone or even the Internet if you are on it. Are you on the Internet? If so, I would also like your e-mail address and would encourage you to get Windows Messenger or something similar so that I could speak to you in such a way. Several of my writers have Messenger, and we find it quite convenient and much quicker than normal mail.

There is much more I would like to discuss with you. Please remember to phone this office as soon as possible, collect if necessary. Again, I am sending this letter overnight express.

Sincerely,
Kate C. Leever
Editor
Roundhouse Publishing Co., Inc.
New York, NY

August 1st
Dear Ms Leever:
   No.
Sincerely,
Lucern Argeneau
Toronto, Ontario

Chapter One

"Rachel swears she never wants to see another coffin as long as she lives."

Lucern grunted at his mother's comment as he and his younger brother Bastien set the coffin down on the basement floor. He knew all about his soon-to-be sister-in-law's new aversion; Etienne had explained everything. That was why he was storing the thing. Etienne was willing to move it out of the mansion to keep his fiancée happy, but for sentimental reasons—he couldn't bring himself to permanently part with it. The man swore he came up with his best ideas lying inside its silent darkness. He was a bit eccentric. He was the only person Lucern could think of who would bring a coffin to his own wedding rehearsal. The minister had been horrified when he'd caught the three brothers transferring it from Etienne's pickup to Bastien's van.

6

"Thank you for driving it over here, Bastien," Lucern said as he straightened.

Bastien shrugged. "You could hardly fit it in your BMW. Besides," he added as they started back up the stairs, "I would rather transport it than store it. My housekeeper would have fits."

Lucern merely smiled. He no longer had a house-keeper to worry about, and the cleaning company he'd hired to drop in once a week only worked on the main floor. Their seeing the coffin wasn't a concern.

"Is everything in place for the wedding?" he asked as he followed his mother and Bastien into the kitchen. He turned out the basement lights and closed the door behind him, but didn't bother turning any other lights on. The weak illumination from the nightlight plugged into the stove was enough to navigate to the front door.

"Yes. Finally." Marguerite Argeneau sounded relieved. "And despite Mrs. Garrett's worries that the wedding was too rushed and that Rachel's family wouldn't have time to arrange to be there, they're all coming."

"How large is the family?" Lucern was sincerely hoping there weren't as many Garretts as there had been Hewitts at Lissianna's wedding. The wedding of his sister to Gregory Hewitt had been a nightmare. The man had a huge family, the majority of which seemed to be female—single females who eyed Lucern, Etienne and Bastien as if they were the main course of a one-course meal. Lucern disliked aggressive women. He'd been born and raised in a time when men were the aggressors and women smiled and simpered and knew their place. He hadn't quite adjusted with the times and wasn't looking forward to another debacle like Lissianna's wedding where he'd spent most of his time avoiding the female guests.

Fortunately, Marguerite soothed some of his fears by announcing, "Rather small compared to Greg's family— and mostly male, from the guest list I saw."

"Thank God," Bastien murmured, exchanging a look with his brother.

Lucern nodded in agreement. "Is Etienne nervous?"

"Surprisingly enough, no." Bastien smiled crookedly. "He's having a great time helping to arrange all this. He swears he can't wait for the wedding day. Rachel seems to make him happy." His expression changed to one of perplexity.

Lucern shared his brother's confusion. He couldn't imagine giving up his freedom to a wife, either. Pausing by the front door, he turned back to find his mother poking through the mail on his hall table.

"Luc, you have unopened mail here from weeks ago! Don't you read it?"

"Why so surprised, mother? He never answers the phone, either. Heck, we're lucky when he bothers to answer the door."

Bastien said the words in a laughing voice, but Lucern didn't miss the exchange of glances between his mother and brother. They were worried about him. He had always been a loner, but lately he had taken that to an extreme and everything seemed a bother. They knew he was growing dangerously bored with life.

"What is this box?"

"I don't know," Lucern admitted as his mother lifted a huge box off the table and shook it as if it were feather-light.

"Well, don't you think it might be a good idea to find out?" she asked impatiently.

Lucern rolled his eyes. No matter how old he got, his mother was likely to interfere and hen-peck. It was something he'd resigned himself to long ago. "I'll get around to it eventually," he muttered. "It's mostly nuisance mail or people wanting something from me."

"What about this letter from your publisher? It's probably important. They wouldn't send it express if it weren't."

Lucern's scowl deepened as his mother picked up the FedEx envelope and turned it curiously in her hands. "It is *not* important. My editor is just harassing me. The company wishes me to do a book-signing tour."

"Edwin wants you to do a book-signing tour?" Marguerite scowled. "I thought you made it clear to him from the start that you weren't interested in publicity."

"Not Edwin. No." Lucern wasn't surprised that his mother recalled his old editor's name; she had a perfect memory and he'd mentioned Edwin many times over the ten years he'd been writing for Roundhouse Publishing. His first works had been published as historical texts used mostly in universities and colleges. Those books were still in use and were celebrated for the fact that they'd been written as if the writer had actually lived through every period about which he wrote. Which, of course, Lucern had. That was hardly public knowledge, though.

Lucern's last three books, however, had been autobiographical in nature. The first told the story of how his mother and father had met and come together, the second how his sister Lissianna had met and fallen in love with her therapist husband, Gregory, and the latest, published just weeks ago, covered the story of his brother Etienne and Rachel Garrett. Lucern hadn't meant to write them, they'd just sort of spilled forth. But once he'd written them, he'd decided they should be published records for the future. Gaining his family's permission, he'd sent them in to Edwin, who'd thought them brilliant works of fiction and published them as such. Not just fiction, either, but "paranormal romance." Lucern had suddenly found himself a romance writer. The whole situation was somewhat distressing for him, so he generally did his best not to think about it.

"Edwin is no longer my editor," he explained. "He had a heart attack late last year and died. His assistant was given his title and position, and she's been harassing me ever since." He scowled again. "The woman is trying to use me to prove herself. She is determined that I should do some publicity events for the novels."

Bastien looked as if he were about to comment, but paused and turned at the sound of a car pulling into the driveway. Lucern opened the door, and the two men watched with varying degrees of surprise as a taxi pulled to a stop beside Bastien's van.

"Wrong address?" Bastien queried, knowing his brother wasn't big on company.

"It must be," Lucern commented. He narrowed his eyes when the driver got out and opened the back door for a young woman.

"Who is that?" Bastien asked. He sounded even more surprised than Lucern felt.

10

"I haven't a clue," Lucern answered. The taxi driver retrieved a small suitcase and overnight bag from the trunk of the car.

"I believe it's your editor," Marguerite announced.

Both Lucern and Bastien swiveled to peer at their mother. They found her reading the now-open FedExed letter.

"My editor? What the hell are you talking about?" Lucern marched over to snatch the letter out of her hand.

Ignoring his rude behavior, Lucern's mother moved to Bastien's side and peered curiously outside. "As the mail is so slow, and because the interest in your books is becoming so widespread, Ms. Kate C. Leever decided to come speak to you in person. Which," Marguerite added archly, "you would know should you bother to read your mail."

Lucern crumpled the letter in his hand. It basically said everything his mother had just verbalized. That, plus the fact that Kate C. Leever would be arriving on the 8 p.m. flight from New York. It was 8:30. The plane must have been on time.

"She's quite pretty, isn't she?" The comment, along with the speculation in his mother's voice when she made it, was enough to raise alarm in Lucern. Marguerite sounded like a mother considering taking the matchmaking trail—a path quite familiar to her. She'd taken it upon first seeing Etienne and Rachel together, too, and look how that had turned out: Etienne hip deep in wedding preparations!

"She's contemplating matchmaking, Bastien. Take her home. Now," Lucern ordered. His brother burst out laughing, moving him to add, "After she has finished

11

with me, she shall focus on finding *you* a wife."

Bastien stopped laughing at once. He grabbed his mother's arm. "Come along, Mother. This is none of our business."

"Of course it is my business." Marguerite shrugged her elbow free. "You are my sons. Your happiness and future are very much my business."

Bastien tried to argue. "I don't understand why this is an issue now. We are both well over four hundred years old. Why, after all this time, have you taken it into your head to see us married off?"

Marguerite pondered for a moment. "Well, ever since your father died, I've been thinking—"

"Dear God," Lucern interrupted. He woefully shook his head.

"What did I say?" his mother asked.

"That is exactly how Lissianna ended up working at the shelter and getting involved with Greg. Dad died, and she started thinking."

Bastien nodded solemnly. "Women shouldn't think."

"Bastien!" Marguerite Argeneau exclaimed.

"Now, now. You know I'm teasing, Mother," he soothed, taking her arm again. This time he got her out the door.

"I, however, am not," Lucern called as he watched them walk down the porch steps to the sidewalk. His mother berated Bastien the whole way, and Lucern grinned at his brother's beleaguered expression. Bastien would catch hell all the way home, Lucern knew, and almost felt sorry for him. Almost.

His laughter died, however, as his gaze switched to the blonde who was apparently his editor. His mother paused in her berating to greet the woman. Lucern almost tried to hear what was said, then decided not to bother. He doubted he wanted to hear it, anyway.

He watched the woman nod and smile at his mother; then she took her luggage in hand and started up the sidewalk. Lucern's eyes narrowed. Dear God, she didn't expect to stay with him, did she? There was no mention in her letter of where she planned to stay. She must expect to stay in a hotel. She would hardly just assume that he would put her up. The woman probably just hadn't stopped at her hotel yet, he reassured himself, his gaze traveling over her person.

Kate C. Leever was about his mother's height, which made her relatively tall for a woman, perhaps 5'10". She was also slim and shapely, with long blond hair. She appeared pretty from the distance presently separating them. In a pale blue business suit, Kate C. Leever resembled a cool glass of ice water. The image was pleasing on this unseasonably warm September evening.

The image shattered when the woman dragged her luggage up the porch steps, paused before him, offered him a bright cheerful smile that lifted her lips and sparkled in her eyes, then blurted, "Hi. I'm Kate Leever. I hope you got my letter. The mail was so slow, and you kept forgetting to send me your phone number, so I thought I'd come visit personally and talk to you about all the publicity possibilities that are opening up for us. I know you're not really interested in partaking of any of them, but I feel sure once I explain the benefits you'll reconsider."

Lucern stared at her wide, smiling lips for one mesmerized moment; then he gave himself a shake. Reconsider? Was that what she wanted? Well, that was easy enough. He reconsidered. It was a quick task.

"No." He closed his door.

Kate stared at the solid wooden panel where Lucern Argeneau's face had been and fought not to shriek with fury. The man was the most difficult, annoying, rude, obnoxious—she pounded on his door—pigheaded, ignorant . . .

The door whipped open, and Kate quickly pasted a blatantly false but wide—she should get high marks for effort—smile on her mouth. The smile nearly slipped when she got a look at him. She hadn't really taken the opportunity earlier. A second before, she had been too busy trying to recall the speech she'd composed and memorized on the flight here; now she didn't have a prepared speech—didn't actually even have a clue what to say—and so she found herself really looking at Lucern Argeneau. The man was a lot younger than she'd expected. Kate knew he'd written for Edwin for a good ten years before she'd taken over working with him, yet he didn't look to be more than thirty-two or-three. That meant he'd been writing professionally since his early twenties.

He was also shockingly handsome. His hair was as dark as night, his eyes a silver blue that almost seemed to reflect the porchlight, his features sharp and strong. He was tall and surprisingly muscular for a man with such a sedentary career. His shoulders bespoke a laborer more than an intellectual. Kate couldn't help but be impressed. Even the scowl on his face didn't detract from his good looks.

14

Without any effort on her part, the smile on Kate's face gained some natural warmth and she said, "It's me again. I haven't eaten yet, and I thought perhaps you'd join me for a meal on the company and we could discuss—"

"No. Please remove yourself from my doorstep." Then Lucern Argeneau closed the door once more.

"Well, that was more than just a 'no'," Kate muttered to herself. "It was even a whole sentence, really." Ever the optimist, she decided to take it as progress.

Raising her hand, she pounded on the door again. Her smile was somewhat battered, but it was still in place when the door opened for the third time. Mr. Argeneau reappeared, looking less pleased than ever to find her still there. This time, he didn't speak but merely arched an eyebrow in question.

Kate supposed that if his speaking a whole sentence was progress, his reverting to complete silence had to be the opposite—but she determined not to think of that. Trying to make her smile a little sunnier, she cleared her throat and said, "If you don't like eating out, perhaps I could order something in and—"

"No." He started to close the door again, but Kate hadn't lived in New York for five years without learning a trick or two. She quickly stuck her foot forward, managing not to wince as the door banged into it and bounced back open.

Before Mr. Argeneau could comment on her guerilla tactics, she said, "If you don't care for takeout, perhaps I could pick up some groceries and cook you something you like." For good measure she added, "That way we could discuss your fears, and I might be able to alleviate them."

He stiffened in surprise at her implication. "I am not afraid," he said.

"I see." Kate allowed a healthy dose of doubt to creep into her voice, more than willing to stoop to manipulation if necessary. Then she waited, foot still in place, hoping that her desperation wasn't showing but knowing that her calm facade was beginning to slip.

The man pursed his lips and took his time considering. His expression made Kate suspect he was measuring her for a coffin, as if he were considering killing her and planting her in his garden to get her out of his hair. She tried not to think about that possibility too hard. Despite having worked with him for years as Edwin's assistant, and now for almost a year as his editor, Kate didn't know the man very well. In her less charitable moments, she *had* considered just what kind of man he might be. Most of her romance authors were female. In fact, *every* other author under her care was female. Lucern Argeneau, who wrote as Luke Amirault, was the only man. What kind of guy wrote romances? And vampire romances at that? She had decided it was probably someone gay . . . or someone weird. His expression at the moment was making her lean toward weird. Serial-killer-type weird.

"You have no intention of removing yourself, do you?" he asked at last.

Kate considered the question. A firm "no" would probably get her inside. But was that what she wanted? Would the man slaughter her? Would she be a headline in the next day's news if she did get in the door?

Cutting off such unproductive and even frightening thoughts, Kate straightened her shoulders and announced firmly; "Mr. Argeneau, I flew up here from New York. This is important to me. I'm determined to talk to you. I'm your *editor*." She emphasized the last word in case he had missed the relevance of that fact. It usually had a certain influence with writers, although Argeneau had shown no signs of being impressed so far.

She didn't know what else to say after that, so Kate simply stood waiting for a response that never came. Heaving a deep sigh, Argeneau merely turned away and started up his dark hall.

Kate stared uncertainly at his retreating back. He hadn't slammed the door in her face this time. That was a good sign, wasn't it? Was it an invitation to enter? Deciding she was going to take it as one, Kate hefted her small suitcase and overnight bag and stepped inside. It was a late-summer evening, cooler than it had been earlier in the day, but still hot. In comparison, stepping into the house was like stepping into a refrigerator. Kate automatically closed the door behind her to keep the cool air from escaping, then paused to allow her eyes to adjust.

The interior of the house was dark. Lucern Argeneau hadn't bothered to turn on any lights. Kate couldn't see much of anything except a square of dim light outlining what appeared to be a door at the end of the long hall in which she stood. She wasn't sure what the light was from; it was too gray and dim to be from an overhead fixture. Kate wasn't even sure that going to that light would bring her to Lucern Argeneau's side, but it was the only source of light she could see, and she was quite sure that it was in the direction he'd taken when walking away.

Setting her bags down by the door, Kate started carefully forward, heading for that square of light, which suddenly seemed so far away. She had no idea if the way was clear or not—she hadn't really looked around before closing the door—but she hoped there was nothing to trip over along the way. If there was, she would certainly find it.

Lucern paused in the center of his kitchen and peered around in the illumination of the nightlight. He wasn't quite sure what to do. He never had guests, or at least hadn't had them for hundreds of years. What did one do with them, exactly? After an inner debate, he moved to the stove, grabbed the teakettle that sat on the burner, and took it to the sink to fill with water. After setting it on the stove and cranking the dial to high, he found the teapot, some tea bags and a full sugar bowl. He set it all haphazardly on a tray.

He would offer Kate C. Leever a cup of tea. Once that was done, so was she.

Hunger drew him to the refrigerator. Light spilled out into the room as he opened the door, making him blink after the previous darkness. Once his eyes adjusted, he bent to pick up one of the two lonely bags of blood on the middle shelf. Other than those bags, there wasn't a single solitary item inside. The cavernous white box was empty. Lucern wasn't much for cooking. His refrigerator had pretty much been empty since his last housekeeper died.

He didn't bother with a glass. Instead, still bent into the fridge, Lucern lifted the blood bag to his mouth and stabbed his fangs into it. The cool elixir of life immediately began to pour into his system, taking the edge off his crankiness. Lucern was never so cranky as when his blood levels were low.

"Mr. Argeneau?"

He jerked in surprise at that query from the doorway. The action ripped the bag he held, sending the crimson fluid spraying out all over him. It squirted in a cold shower over his face and into his hair as he instinctively straightened and banged his head on the underside of the closed freezer compartment. Cursing, Lucern dropped the ruined bag onto the refrigerator shelf and grabbed for his head with one hand, slamming the refrigerator door closed with the other.

Kate Leever rushed to his side. "Oh, my goodness! Oh! I'm so sorry! *Oh!*" she screeched as she caught sight of the blood coating his face and hair. "Oh, God! You've cut your head. *Bad!*"

Lucern hadn't seen an expression of such horror on anyone's face since the good old days when lunch meant biting into a nice warm neck rather than a nasty cold bag.

Seeming to recover her senses somewhat, Kate Leever grabbed his arm and urged him toward the kitchen table. "Here, you'd better sit down. You're bleeding badly."

"I am fine," Lucern muttered as she settled him into a chair. He found her concern rather annoying. If she was too nice to him, he might feel guilted into being nice back.

"Where's your phone?" She was turning on one heel, scanning the kitchen for the item in question.

"Why do you wish a phone?" he asked hopefully.

19

Perhaps she would leave him alone now, he thought briefly, but her answer nixed that possibility.

"To call an ambulance. You really hurt yourself."

Her expression became more distressed as she looked at him again, and Lucern found himself glancing down at his front. There was quite a bit of blood on his shirt, and he could feel it streaming down his face. He could also smell it—sharp and rich with tinny overtones. Without thinking, he slid his tongue out to lick his lips. Then what she'd said slipped into his mind, and he straightened abruptly. While it was convenient that she thought the blood was from an injury, there was no way he was going to a hospital.

"I am fine. I do not need medical assistance," he announced firmly.

"What?" She peered at him with disbelief. "There's blood everywhere! You really hurt yourself."

"Head wounds bleed a lot." He gave a dismissive wave, then stood and moved to the sink to rinse off. If he didn't wash quickly, he was going to shock the woman by licking the blood off his hands all the way up to his elbows. The bit he'd managed to consume before she startled him had barely eased his hunger at all.

"Head wounds may bleed a lot, but this is—"

Lucern gave a start as Kate suddenly stepped to his side and grabbed his head. He was so surprised that he bent dutifully at her urging . . . until she said, "I can't see—"

He straightened the moment he realized what she was doing, then quickly bent over the sink to duck his head under the tap so she couldn't get at his head again and see that there was no wound.

"I am fine. I clot quickly," he said as cold water splashed on his head and ran over his face.

Kate Leever had no answer to that, but Lucern could feel her standing at his back watching. Then she moved to his side, and he felt her warm body press against him as she bent to try to examine his head again.

For a moment, Lucern was transfixed. He was terribly aware of her body so close, of the heat pouring off her, of her sweet scent. For that moment, his hunger became confused. It wasn't the smell of the blood pulsing in her veins that filled his nostrils, it was a whiff of spice and flowers and her own personal scent. It filled his head, clouding his thoughts. Then he became aware of her hands moving through his hair under the tap, searching for a wound she wouldn't find, and he jerked upward in an attempt to stand away from her. The attempt was neatly thwarted by the tap slamming into the back of his head. Pain shattered through him, and water squirted everywhere, sending Kate stepping back with a squeal.

Cursing, Lucern ducked out from under the tap and snatched at the first thing to come to hand; a tea towel. He wrapped it around his wet head, straightened, then pointed at the door. "Out of my kitchen. Out!"

Kate C. Leever blinked in surprise at his return of temper, then seemed to grow an inch in height as she marshaled her own. Her voice was firm as she said, "You need a doctor."

"No."

Her eyes narrowed. "Is that the only word you know?"

"No."

She threw her hands up in the air, then let them drop—as quick as that, seeming to relax. Lucern found himself wary.

Kate C. Leever smiled and moved to finish making the tea he had started. "That settles it, then," she said.

"Settles what?" Lucern asked, watching suspiciously as she threw the two teabags in the tea pot and poured hot water over them.

Kate shrugged mildly and set the kettle back. "I had intended on trying to talk to you, then checking into a hotel later tonight. However, now that you've hurt yourself and refuse to go the hospital . . ." She turned away from the steeping tea to raise one eyebrow. "You won't reconsider?"

"No."

She nodded and turned back to plop the lid again on the teapot. The clink it made had an oddly satisfied sound to it as she explained, "I can't leave you alone after such an injury. Head wounds are tricky. I suppose I shall have to stay here."

Lucern was opening his mouth to let her know that she most certainly was not staying there, when she moved toward the refrigerator and asked, "Do you take milk?"

Recalling the bag of blood ripped open in the fridge, he raced past her and threw himself wildly in front of her. "No!"

She stared at him, mouth agape, until he realized he stood before the refrigerator door with his arms widespread in a panicked pose. He immediately shifted to lean against it, arms and ankles crossed in a position he hoped appeared more natural. Then he glared at her for good measure. It had the effect of making her close her mouth; then she said uncertainly, "Oh. Well, I do. If you have any."

"No."

She nodded slowly, but concern filled her face and she actually lifted a hand to place it soft and warm against his forehead as if checking for fever. Lucern inhaled the scent of her and felt his stance relax somewhat.

"Are you sure you won't go to the hospital?" Kate asked. "You're acting a tad strange, and head wounds really aren't something to mess with."

"No."

Lucern was alarmed when he heard how low his voice had gone. He was even more concerned when Kate Leever smiled and asked teasingly, "Now, why aren't I surprised by that answer?"

Much to his dismay, he almost smiled back at her. Catching himself, he scowled harder instead and berated himself for his momentary weakness. Kate C. Leever, editor, might be being nice to him right now, but that was only because she wanted something from him. And he would do well to remember that.

"Well, come along, then."

Lucern stopped his woolgathering to note that his editor had collected the tea tray and was moving toward the kitchen door.

"We should move to the living room, where you can sit down for a bit. You took quite a blow," she added as she pushed through the swinging door with one hip.

Lucern took a step after her, then paused to glance

23

back at the refrigerator, his thoughts on the other full bag of blood inside. It was his last until the fresh delivery tomorrow night. He was terribly hungry, almost faint with it. Which was no doubt the reason behind his weakness in the face of Kate C. Leever's steamroller approach. Perhaps just a sip would strengthen him for the conversation ahead. He reached for the door.

"Lucern?"

He stiffened at that call. When had she stopped addressing him as Mr. Argeneau? And why did his name on her lips sound so sexy? He really needed to feed. He pulled the refrigerator door open and reached for the bag.

"Lucern?" There was concern in her voice this time, and she sounded closer. She must be coming back. No doubt she feared he had passed out from his injury.

He released a mutter of frustration and closed the refrigerator door. The last thing he needed was another debacle like spilling blood all over himself. That had already caused him unending problems, like the fact that the woman now planned to stay with him. He'd meant to nix the idea at once, but had been distracted by Ms. Leever approaching the refrigerator. *Damn!*

Well, he would straighten her out on that issue first thing. He'd be damned if he was letting her stay here and harangue him about all this publicity nonsense. That was that. He would be firm. Cruel, if necessary. She wasn't staying here.

Lucern tried to get rid of her, but Kate C. Leever was rather like a bulldog once she made up her mind about something. No, a bulldog was the wrong image. A terrier perhaps. Yes, he was happier with that comparison. A cute blond terrier hanging off of his arm, teeth sunk determinedly into the cuff of his shirt and refusing to let go. Short of smashing her against the wall a couple of times, he really had no idea how to get her jaws off him.

It was the situation of course. Despite having lived for several hundred years, Lucern had failed to come up against anything of the sort. In his experience, people were a bother and never failed to bring chaos with them. Women especially. He'd always been a sucker for a damsel in distress. He couldn't recount how many times he'd found himself stumbling across a woman with troubles and suddenly finding his whole life in turmoil while he fought a battle, a duel, or a war for her. Of course, he always won and saved the day. Still, somehow he never got the woman. In the end, all his efforts and the upheavals in his life left him watching the woman walk away with someone else.

That wasn't the situation here. Kate C. Leever, editor, was not a damsel in distress. In fact, she apparently saw *him* as the one in distress. She was staying "for his own good." She was saving him, in her mind, and intended to "wake him every hour on the hour should he fall asleep," to save him from his own foolishness in refusing to go to the doctor. She made that announcement the moment they were seated in his living room, then calmly set about removing the tea bags from the pot and pouring tea while he gaped at her.

Lucern didn't need her help. He hadn't really hit his head that hard, and even if he had, his body would have repaired itself quickly. But that wasn't something he could tell the woman. In the end, he simply said, with all the sternness and firmness he could muster, "I do not desire your help, Ms. Leever. I can take care of myself."

She nodded sedately, sipped her tea, then smiled pleasantly and said, "I would take that comment much more seriously were you not presently wearing a pretty but bloodstained flowered tea towel on your head . . . turban style."

Lucern reached up in alarm, only to feel the tea towel he'd forgotten was wrapped around his head. As he began to unravel it, Kate added, "Don't remove it on my account. It looks rather adorable on you and makes you far less intimidating."

Lucern growled. He ripped the flowered tea towel off.

"What was that?" his editor asked, eyes wide. "You growled."

"I did not."

"You did so." She was grinning widely, looking very pleased. "Oh, you men are so cute."

Lucern knew then that the battle was lost. There would be no argument that would make her leave.

Perhaps mind control . . .

It was a skill he tried to avoid using as a rule, and hadn't exercised in some time. It wasn't usually necessary, since the family had switched to utilizing a blood bank for feeding rather than hunting. But this occasion clearly called for it.

As he watched Kate sip her tea, he tried to get into her thoughts so that he might take control of them. He was beyond shocked to find only a blank wall. Kate C.

Leever's mind was as inaccessible to him as if a door had been closed and locked. Still, he continued to try for several moments, his lack of success more alarming than he would have expected.

He didn't give up until she broke the silence by bringing up her reason for being there: "Perhaps we could now discuss the book-signing tour."

Lucern reacted as if she'd poked him with a hot iron. Giving up on controlling her mind and making her leave, he leapt to his feet. "There are three guest rooms. They're upstairs, all three on the left. My room and office are on the right. Stay out of them. Take whichever of the guest rooms you want."

Then he retreated from the battlefield with all haste, rushing back to the kitchen.

He could put up with her for one night, he told himself. Once the night was over and she was reassured that he was fine, she would leave. He would see to that.

Trying not to recall that he'd been just as determined and certain about expelling her after she finished her tea, Lucern snatched a glass and his last bag of blood from the fridge. Then he moved to the sink to pour himself some dinner. He could probably get a quick cup while Ms. Kate C. Leever was occupied in choosing a room.

He'd thought wrong. Lucern had just started to pour the blood from its bag to the glass when the kitchen door opened behind him.

"Do you have any all-night grocery stores in town?"

Dropping the glass and bag, Lucern whirled to face her, wincing as the glass smashed in the sink.

"I'm sorry, I didn't mean to startle you, I . . ." She

paused when he held up a hand to halt her forward progress.

"Just . . ." he began, then finished wearily; "What did you ask?"

He couldn't really listen to her answer. The sweet, tinny scent of blood seemed rich in the air, though he doubted Kate could smell it from where she was across the room. It was distracting, and even more distracting was the rushing sound of it all running out of the bag and down the sink. His dinner. His last bag.

His mind was screaming NO! His body was cramping in protest. That being the case, Kate C. Leever's words sounded like "Blah blah blah" as she moved toward his empty refrigerator and peered inside. Lucern didn't bother to stop her this time. Apart from the blood from earlier, it was completely empty. However, he did try to concentrate on what she was saying, hoping that the sooner he dealt with her question, the sooner he could save his dinner. Try as he might, however, he was really only catching a word here and there.

"Blah blah blah . . . haven't eaten since breakfast. Blah blah blah . . . really don't have anything here. Blah blah blah . . . shopping?"

The last chorus of blahs ended on a high note, alerting Lucern to the fact that it had been a question. He wasn't sure what the question was, but he could sense that a no would probably provoke an argument.

"Yes," he blurted, hoping to be rid of the stubborn woman. Much to his relief, the answer pleased her and sent her back to the hall door.

"Blah blah blah . . . pick my room."

28

He could almost taste the blood, its scent was so heavy in the air.

"Blah blah . . . change into something more comfortable."

He was starving.

"Blah blah be right back and we can go."

The door closed behind her, and Lucern whirled back to the sink. He moaned. The bag was almost completely drained. It was flat. Nearly. Feeling somewhat desperate, he picked it up, tipped it over his mouth and squeezed, trying to wring out the last few drops. He got exactly three before giving up and tossing the bag into the garbage with disgust. If there had been any question before, there wasn't now. Without a doubt, Kate C. Leever was going to make his life a living hell until she left. He just knew it.

And what the heck had he agreed to anyway?

Chapter Two

"Shopping!"

Kate laughed at Lucern's disgusted mutter as they entered the 24-hour grocery store. He'd been repeating it every few minutes since leaving the house. At first he'd said the word as if he couldn't believe he'd agreed to go. Then, as they'd driven here in his BMW, that dismay had turned to disgust. You'd think the man had never gone food shopping before now! Of course, judging by how empty his cupboards were, Kate supposed he hadn't. And when she'd commented on the lack of food in his home on the way out of the house, he'd muttered something about not having replaced his housekeeper yet. Kate presumed that meant he ate out a lot in the meantime.

She hadn't bothered to inquire as to what had become of his previous housekeeper. His personality was answer enough. No doubt the poor woman had quit. Kate herself would have, she knew.

She led him to the rows of empty shopping carts. As she started to pull one out, Lucern grunted something that might have been "Allow me," but could just as easily have been "Get the hell out of the way." He then took over the chore,

In Kate's experience, men always preferred to do the driving—whether it was a car, a golf cart, or a shopping basket. She suspected it was a control issue, but either way it was handy; it meant she was free to fill the thing up.

She began to make a mental list of what she should get as she led the way toward the dairy section. She would have to be sure she got lots of fruits and vegetables for Lucern. The man was big and muscular, but far too pale. It seemed obvious to her that he was in dire need of some green leafy vegetables.

Maybe vegetables would improve his mood, too.

Lucern needed blood. That was the one thought pulsing through his mind as he followed Kate C. Leever through the dairy section, the frozen-food section, and now down the coffee aisle. The cart was filling up quickly. Kate had already tossed various yogurts, cheeses, eggs and a ton of frozen gourmet dinners in it. Now she paused in the coffee aisle and considered the various packages before turning to ask, "What brand do you prefer?"

He stared at her blankly. "Brand?"

"Of coffee? What do you normally drink?"

Lucern shrugged. "I do not drink coffee."

"Oh. Tea, then?"

"I do not drink tea."

"But you—," She narrowed her eyes. "Hot chocolate? Espresso? Capuccino?" When he shook his head at all her suggestions, she asked with exasperation: "Well, what *do* you drink then? Kool-Aid?"

A titter of amusement drew Lucern's attention to a plump young woman pushing a cart up the aisle toward them. She was the first shopper they'd come across since entering the store. Between the debacles with the blood bags, the tea in the living room, and the bit of time Kate had taken to settle in and change, it was now nearly midnight. The grocery store wasn't very busy at this hour.

Now that her giggle had caught his attention, the shopper batted her eyelashes at Lucern and he found himself smiling back, his gaze fixed on the pulse at the base of her throat. He imagined sinking his teeth there and drawing the warm, sweet blood out of her. She was his favorite sort to drink. Plump, pink women always had the best, richest blood. Thick and heady and—

"Mr. Argeneau? Earth calling Lucern!"

Luc's pleasant imaginings shattered. He turned reluctantly back to his editor. "Yes?"

"What do you like to drink?" she repeated.

He glanced back at the shopper. "Er . . . coffee's fine."

"You said you don't drink cof—Never mind. What brand?"

Lucern surveyed the choices. His eyes settled on a dark red can with the name Tim Hortons. He'd always thought that was a donut shop or something. Still, it was the only name he recognized, so he pointed at it.

"The most expensive one, of course," Kate muttered. She picked up a can of fine grind.

Lucern hadn't noticed the price. "Stop complaining. I am paying for the groceries."

"No. I said I'd pay and I will."

Had she said she'd pay when she'd mentioned it earlier? he wondered. He couldn't recall; he hadn't been paying much attention at the time. His thoughts had been on other things. Like the blood dripping down the sink and not into his parched mouth.

His gaze slid back to the plump, pulsing-veined shopper who continued past him. He imagined he looked like a starving man watching a buffet being wheeled past. He was hard-pressed not to throw himself onto it. Warm, fresh blood . . . much nicer than that cold bagged stuff he and his family had taken to ingesting. He hadn't realized how much he missed the old-fashioned way of feeding.

"Lucern?" There was a touch of irritation in Kate Leever's voice, and it made him scowl as he turned back. She wasn't where she'd last stood, but had moved on down the aisle and was waiting for him. She wore an annoyed expression, which in turn annoyed him. What did *she* have to be irritable about? She wasn't the one starving.

Then he had a vague recollection of her saying she hadn't eaten since breakfast, and he supposed she was hungry too and therefore had just as much right to be grouchy. It was a grudging admission.

"*I* am paying," he announced firmly as he pushed the cart forward. "You are a guest in my home. I will feed you." As opposed to feeding on you, he thought, which was what he most wanted to do. Well, not what he *most* wanted to do. He'd rather feed on the plump little brunette behind him. He had always found the blood of sleek, blond creatures like Kate C. Leever to be thin and bland. Plump-girl blood was better-tasting, more flavorful, fuller-bodied.

Of course, he couldn't feed on anyone. It was too dangerous nowadays, and even if he himself was willing to take the risk, he wouldn't risk the safety of his family just for a few moments of culinary pleasure.

It didn't mean he couldn't dream about it, though, so Lucern spent the next few moments trailing Kate around the canned food and dry goods aisles, absently agreeing with everything she said while he fondly recalled meals he'd enjoyed in the past.

"Do you like Mexican?" she asked.

"Oh, yes," he murmured, the question immediately bringing to mind a perky little Mexican girl he'd feasted on in Tampico. She'd been a tasty little bundle. Warm and sweet-smelling in his arms, little enjoyable moans issuing from her throat as he'd plunged both his body and teeth into her . . . Oh, yes. Feeding could be a full-body experience.

"What about Italian?"

"Italian is delicious too," he said agreeably, his memories immediately switching to a pleasing little peasant on the Amalfi coast. That had been his first feeding on his own. A man always remembered his first. And just the thought of his sweet little Maria made him warm all over. Such deep, dark eyes and long, wavy, midnight hair. He recalled tangling his hands in that hair and the deep groan of pleasure she'd breathed into his ear as he'd given her his virginity and taken her blood at the same time. Truly, it had been a sweet and memorable experience.

"Do you like steak?"

Lucern was once again drawn from his thoughts, this time by a package of raw meat suddenly shoved under his nose, interrupting his fond memories. It was steak, nice and bloody, and though he normally preferred human blood—even cold bagged human blood to bovine—the blood-soaked steak smelled good at the moment. He found himself inhaling deeply and letting his breath out on a slow sigh.

The package was jerked away. "Or do you prefer white meat?"

"Oh, no. No. Red meat is better." He moved closer to the meat counter she'd led him to and peered around with his first real interest since they'd entered the market. He had always been a meat-and-potatoes man. Rare meat, as a rule.

"A carnivore, I take it," Kate commented dryly as he reached for a particularly bloody package of steak. The blood was dripping, and he almost licked his lips. Then, afraid he might do something distressing in his present state, like lick the package, he stepped back and set the meat down. Taking hold of the cart, he began moving it along, hoping to get to a less tempting section.

"Hang on," Kate called, but Lucern kept walking, almost moaning when she rushed up with several packages of steak in her arms that she dumped in the cart.

Great! Now the temptation would follow him. He really needed to feed. He had to contact Bastien or Etienne and see about borrowing some blood. Perhaps

35

he could make a quick stop at Bastien's on the way home. He could leave the unshakable Kate Leever in the car with the groceries, run in, gulp down a bit of nourishment and . . .

Dear God! He sounded like a junkie!

"Fruits and vegetables next, I think," Kate said beside him. "You're obviously in serious need of vitamins. Have you ever considered going to a tanning salon?"

"I can't. I have an . . . er, skin condition. And I'm allergic to the sun, too."

"That must make life difficult at times," she commented. Peering at him wide-eyed she asked, "Is that why you are so difficult about book signings and other promo stuff?"

He shrugged. As she began picking up all sorts of green things, he grimaced. In defense, he picked up a twenty-pound bag of potatoes to fill the cart, but it was soon covered in green: little round green things, big round green things, long green stalks. Dear God, the woman had a green fetish!

Lucern started moving the cart along a little more quickly, forcing Kate to hurry as she started on other colors. Orange, red and yellow vegetables flew into the cart and were followed by orange, red and purple fruit before Lucern managed to at last force her to the cash register.

The moment he stopped the cart, Kate began throwing things on the conveyor belt. He was watching her absently when the plump shopper pushed her cart by. She smiled and batted her eyelashes again, then gave him a little wave. Lucern smiled back, his gaze affixed to the pulse beating in her neck. He could practically hear the *thump-thump* of her heart, the rushing sound of blood, the—

"Lucern? Mr. Argeneau. Where are you going?"

Pausing, Lucern blinked his eyes, realizing only at Kate's question that he'd started to follow the plump shopper like a horse walking after a dangling carrot. His possible dinner looked back and smiled again before disappearing down the frozen-foods aisle. Lucern started after her. "We forgot ice cream."

"Ice cream?" He heard the confusion in Kate's voice, but he couldn't have stopped to answer had he wished. He hurried to the frozen-foods aisle only to find another shopper there in addition to his plump lovely. They hadn't crossed paths with any but the plump shopper all night, yet now there was another one present, hindering him from a quick bite! Sighing inwardly, he moved to the ice cream section and glanced distractedly, over the options. Chocolate, cherry, Rocky Road.

He glanced toward his plump lovely. She was watching him and giving coquettish smiles. She looked like a big, smiling steak on legs. Damned woman! It's not nice to tease, he thought unhappily and opened the cooler wider as he stared.

She approached, smiling widely as he pulled ice cream out of the cooler. She didn't say a word, just smiled naughtily as she walked past, her arm brushing against him.

Lucern inhaled deeply, nearly dizzy from the scent of her. Oh yes, her blood was sweet. Or was that the ice cream he held? He grabbed another carton and watched her disappear around the corner with a sigh. He wanted to follow. He could use his brain-control trick to lure her into the back of the store for a little suck. But if he was caught . . .

Sighing, he gave up on the idea and grabbed some Rocky Road ice cream. He could hold out a little while longer. Just a little while more, and he would be free to escape to Bastien's or Etienne's. Surely Kate C. Leever was exhausted after her workday and flight, and would want to make a night of it.

"My, you do like ice cream," Kate commented as he returned.

Lucern glanced down at the four cartons he held and dumped them onto the conveyor belt with a shrug. He had no idea what flavors several of them were, and in his distraction hadn't even realized he'd grabbed so many, but it didn't matter. They'd get eaten eventually.

Kate protested his paying, but Lucern insisted. It was a man thing. His pride wouldn't allow a woman to pay for food intended for his home. Kate opened a bag of rice cakes to munch on the way back. She offered him some, but he merely sneered and shook his head. Rice cakes. Dear God.

Lucern managed to not stop at either of his brothers' houses. He was rather proud of his self-restraint. He and Kate carted the groceries inside his home; then he insisted she start cooking while he put them away. This made him look helpful and useful, when in truth he just wanted her to cook her damned meal, eat it, and go to bed so that he could go in search of what he needed. Not that he couldn't enjoy food, too. A little food wouldn't go amiss, but regular food wouldn't help his main hunger. His people could survive without food, but not without blood.

38

Fortunately, Kate C. Leever was apparently ravenous, because she made a quick meal, grilling a couple of steaks and then throwing together a bowl of a bunch of green stuff with some sort of sauce on it. Lucern had never seen the attraction of salads. Rabbits ate greens. Humans ate meat, and Lucern ate meat and blood. He was not a rabbit. However, he kept his opinions to himself and finished up with the unpacking at nearly the same time as Kate finished cooking; then they sat down to eat.

Lucern dug into his steak with fervor, ignoring the rabbit bowl. He'd asked for the meat rare, and he supposed it was rare to most people—but rare to him was *rare*. Still, it was tender and juicy, and he ate it quickly.

He watched Kate finish, but shook his head when she offered him salad. "You really should eat some," she lectured with a frown. "It's full of vitamins and nutrients, and you're still awfully pale."

He presumed she feared that his pallor was due to his supposed head injury. It was due to lack of blood, however, which reminded Lucern that he should see if Bastien was home. Excusing himself, he left the room and went to his office.

Much to his disappointment, when he called his brother, there was no answer. Bastien was either out on a date or had gone back to Argeneau Industries. Like Lucern, Bastien preferred working at night when everyone else was sleeping. The habits of a couple hundred years were hard to break.

Lucern returned to the kitchen, to find that Kate Leever had finished eating and had already rinsed off most of the dishes and set them in the dishwasher.

"I shall finish that," he said at once. "You must be exhausted and ready for bed."

Kate glanced at Lucern with surprise. It was hard to believe this was the same man who had written those short "nos" in response to her letters and been so rude when she'd first arrived. His helping her unload groceries and apparent consideration now made her suspicious. The hopeful look on his face didn't help much, either. However, she *was* tired. It had been a long day, so she reluctantly admitted, "I am tired, actually."

In the next moment, she found her arm grasped in a firm hand and herself being propelled out of the kitchen.

"It's to bed with you!" Argeneau sounded cheerful at the prospect, and he rushed her up the hall and then the stairs. "Sleep as late as you like. I shall probably work all night as usual and sleep most of the day. If you rise before me, eat whatever you wish, drink whatever you wish, but *do not poke around.*" The last was said in a hard tone that sounded more like the rude man she expected.

"I would hardly poke around," she said quickly, annoyed. "I brought a manuscript with me to edit. I'll just do that until you get up."

"Good, good. Good night." He pushed her into the yellow guest room she'd chosen earlier and pulled the door closed with a snap.

Kate turned slowly toward it, almost expecting to hear the door's lock click into place. She was relieved when that didn't happen. Shaking her head at her own suspicious mind, she moved to her suitcase to find her nightgown, then went into the en suite bathroom to shower. She was just crawling into bed when she recalled the excuse she'd used to get to stay here. She paused to glance around.

Spotting the small digital clock on the bedside table, she picked it up and set it to ring in an hour. She had every intention of getting up to check to be sure that Lucern hadn't fallen asleep—and that if he had, he could still wake up.

Kate set the alarm back on the table and crawled under the covers, thinking of those few panicked moments in the kitchen. She drew a deep breath through her nose, recalling Lucern Argeneau standing before her, blood streaming down his head and face. Dear God, she'd never actually seen a head injury before. She'd heard they could be bloody, of course, and that they often looked worse than they truly were, but there had been so much blood.

She shuddered and swallowed a knot of anxiety. Kate hardly knew the man, and he'd been nothing but rude to her since her arrival, but despite the fact that it would serve him right after his behavior, she really didn't want to see him dead. How was she going to impress her boss that way? She could see it now. "No, Allison, I wasn't able to convince him to do the newspaper interviews. No, nor the television shows. Er . . . no, he won't be doing signings either. Actually, I might have been able to convince him, except I killed him instead. It was an accident, Allison. I know he is our latest cash cow, and I truly didn't mean to kill him despite the fact that he's a rude, pigheaded . . . No, really, it was an accident! Yes, I do realize I'm fired. No, I don't blame you at all for not giving me a reference. Yes, if

41

you'll excuse me I'll just go apply at McDonald's now that my publishing career is ruined."

Sighing, she shook her head on the pillow and closed her eyes. Thank goodness Argeneau seemed healthy— except for the pallor. She sat up in bed, concern eating at her again. He really had been awfully pale.

"And why not?" she asked herself. It looked as if he'd lost a quart of blood. Or at least a pint. Maybe she should check on him now. Kate considered the matter briefly, partly wanting to check on him, partly reluctant to have him bark at her for interrupting him at whatever he was doing. He was surely going to bark enough when she checked on him every hour through the night. But he had been terribly pale after hitting his head.

On the other hand, she had noticed his pallor on the porch before he'd ever hit his head. Or had that been the lighting? It had been nighttime, and the light on the porch had been one of those neon jobbies. That might have simply made him appear pale.

She mulled over the matter briefly, started to slip her feet off the bed to go check on him before she went to sleep, but then she paused at the sound of a closing door. Stiffening, Kate listened to the soft pad of feet down the hall, then forced herself to relax and lie back down. The footsteps had been soft, but otherwise normal. Lucern didn't sound to be staggering or unduly slow. He was fine. She would stick to her plan to check him in an hour.

Relaxing, she lay back and closed her eyes. She wasn't going to get much sleep tonight and knew it. In truth, she'd really rather be in a hotel somewhere sleeping soundly. And she would be—head wound or no head wound—if she weren't so afraid that once he got her out of the house, Lucern Argeneau wasn't likely to let her back in. Kate couldn't risk that; she just *had* to convince him to do one of the publicity appearances. Any one of them would do. She very much feared that keeping her new position as editor depended on it.

"You're kidding? She really thought all that blood was from a little bump on the head?" Etienne gave a disbelieving laugh.

"Well, she would hardly imagine it came from a bag of blood in his fridge," Bastien pointed out, but he was chuckling too.

Lucern ignored his brothers' amusement and sank his teeth into the second bag of blood Rachel brought him. He'd already ingested the first. He had insisted on doing so before explaining why he'd shown up at Etienne's home pleading to be fed. The first bag had allowed him to get over his surprise that Bastien was there. It had also given his brothers time to explain that Bastien had come by to help sort out some last-minute problems with the wedding. Which explained nicely why Lucern hadn't been able to reach him.

"What I don't understand," Bastien said as Lucern finished off the second bag and retracted his teeth, "is why you didn't simply get into her head and suggest she leave."

"I tried," Lucern admitted wearily. He placed both empty bags in the hand Rachel held out, then watched her walk out of the room to dispose of them. "But I could not get into her mind."

The silence that followed was as effective as great gusty gasps would have been from anyone else. Etienne and Bastien stared at him, stunned.

"You're kidding," Bastien said at last.

When Lucern shook his head, Etienne dropped onto the chair across from him and said, "Well, don't tell Mother if you don't want her pushing you two together. The minute she heard that I couldn't read Rachel's mind was the minute she decided we'd make a good couple." He paused thoughtfully. "Of course, she *was* right."

Lucern grunted in digust. "Well, Ms. Kate C. Leever is not perfect for me. The woman is as annoying as a gnat flying about your head. Stubborn as a mule, and pushy as hell. The damned woman has not given me a moment's peace since pushing her way over my doorstep."

"Not true," Bastien argued with amusement. "You managed to give her the slip long enough to come here."

"That is only because she was tired and went to bed. She . . ." He paused suddenly and sat up straight, recalling her promise to check on him every hour to be sure his head injury hadn't done more damage than he believed. Would she really do that? He glanced sharply at his brothers. "How long have I been here?"

Bastien's eyebrows rose curiously, but he glanced at his watch and said: "I'm not positive, but I'd guess you've been here about forty, forty-five minutes."

"Damn." Lucern was on his feet at once and heading for the door. "I have to go. My thanks for the drinks, Rachel," he called loudly at the other room.

44

"Wait. What . . . ?"

Bastien and Etienne got up to follow, questions slipping from their lips, but Lucern didn't stop to answer. He'd locked his office door before leaving the house, and Kate might assume that meant he was in there, but if she really did check on him hourly and got no answer when she knocked on the door, the damned woman might decide he'd died or something and call the police or an ambulance. She might even break down his office door herself. There was just no telling what that woman might do.

He came up with a couple of doozies as he hurried home.

Fortunately, she hadn't done any of them by the time he returned. She was up and trying to rouse him, though—that much was obvious the moment he opened the front door. He could hear her shouting and banging on his office door all the way downstairs. Rolling his eyes at the racket she was making and the panic in her voice as she called his name, Lucern pocketed his house keys and jogged upstairs. He came to an abrupt halt at the top of the steps.

Dear God, the woman didn't just eat rabbit food, she wore rabbit slippers.

Lucern gawked at the ears flopping over the furry pink bunny slippers she wore, then let his gaze slide up over her heavy, also pink and fuzzy, housecoat. If he didn't already know she had a nice figure, he wouldn't know now. Then he caught a glimpse of her hair and winced. She'd gone to bed with wet hair and had obviously tossed around a lot in her sleep; her hair was standing on end in every direction.

On the bright side, she obviously didn't intend on stooping to seducing him into doing any of those publicity things she was so fired up for him to do. Oddly enough, Lucern actually felt a touch of regret at that realization. He didn't understand why. He didn't even like the woman. Still, he might have been open to a little seduction.

"Good evening," he said when she paused in her yelling to take a breath. He found himself gaping again, as Kate C. Leever whirled around to face him.

"You! I thought . . ." She turned to the locked office door, then back to him. "This door is locked. I thought you were in there, and when you didn't answer, I . . ." Her voice trailed away as she took in his expression. Suddenly self-conscious, she pulled the edges of her ratty old robe together as if he might be trying to catch a better look at the flannel nightgown showing at the neckline. "Is something wrong?"

Lucern couldn't help it; he knew it was rude, but he couldn't stop the words from blurting through his lips. "Dear God! What is that goop on your face?"

Kate immediately let go of her robe and pressed both hands to her face, her mouth forming an alarmed "Oh" as she recalled and tried to hide the dry green mask.

It was obviously some sort of beauty treatment, Lucern deduced, but Kate didn't stick around to explain exactly what sort. Turning on her heel, she fled back to the guest room and closed the door. After a heartbeat, she called in a strained voice, "I'm glad you're all right. Mostly. I was worried when you didn't answer my knock. I'll check on you again in an hour."

Silence then filled the hall.

Lucern waited a moment, but when he didn't hear the sound of footsteps moving away from the door, he decided she was waiting for some sort of response. "*No*" was the first response that came to mind. He didn't want her checking on him. He didn't want her here at all. But he found he couldn't tell her that. She'd appeared terribly embarrassed to be caught looking as she had, and really he couldn't blame her; she'd looked awful in a cute, bunny type way.

He smiled to himself at the memory of her standing there in his hall looking like hell. Kate *had* looked bad—but in the sort of adorable way that made him want to hug her . . . until he'd seen the cracking green mask on her face.

Lucern decided not to further distress her with the "no" she no doubt expected and instead called out "Good-night" in an uncomfortably gruff voice. As he moved to his office door and unlocked it, he heard a little sigh from the other side of her door, then a very small "good-night" in return. Her soft footsteps padded away. She was going to bed, he thought.

There came a snap, and light fingered its way out from under the guest room door. Lucern paused. Why were the lights on? Was she resetting her alarm clock for an hour from now? The silly woman really did intend to check on him every hour!

Shaking his head, he stepped into his office and flicked on the lights. He'd give her fifteen minutes to fall asleep and then go in and turn off the alarm clock. The last thing he needed was for her to be pestering him all night. Although it did occur to him that if she didn't sleep much tonight, she would probably sleep longer in the morning to make up for it, which would give her less time to nose around on her own while he was sleeping.

No, he decided. She'd said she wouldn't poke around, and he believed her.

Mostly.

Chapter Three

Kate poked around.

She didn't mean to. In fact, she had made plans for the day which definitely did not include poking around—but, well, the best-laid plans and all that. They always went awry.

Kate woke up at ten a.m. Her first thought was to wonder where she was. Her second thought—once she recalled where she was and why—was "Oh, shit, the alarm didn't go off." Sitting up in bed, she reached for the alarm clock to look it over. It was set to the off position. Kate frowned at the thing, sure she had reset it after checking on Lucern the first time. She distinctly recalled resetting it and turning it on. But it was off. She set it back with a frown. Had she woken up the second time just to roll over and turn it off? That must be it, she realized and grimaced to herself.

"Way to go, Leever. The one excuse you had to stay here, the one opportunity to ingratiate yourself with the

49

man, and you blew it." Her thinking had been that surely he couldn't oust her after she'd gone to the trouble of rousing herself every hour to be sure he was all right. But now that she'd failed at her task, he'd have her out of there by noon—if he hadn't written all night as he'd claimed he was going to do. If he had written all night, he might not wake up until two or three o'clock. Which meant she'd be out of there by three or four.

"Good show, Katie." She pushed the bedsheet aside and slipped out of bed. Now she'd have to come up with another good excuse to stay until she convinced Lucern Argeneau to cooperate.

Kate pondered the problem while she showered, while she dried off, while she dressed, while she brushed her teeth, while she fiddled with her hair and while she dabbed on a touch of face powder. At last she gave it up as a lost cause until after she'd eaten. She always thought better on a full stomach.

Leaving the guest room, she paused in the hallway and stared at the door opposite her own. Maybe she should check on her host. She hadn't done her checking through the night. The man might be lying comatose on his office floor.

She pursed her lips thoughtfully over the matter, then shook her head. Nope. Not a good idea, she decided. She'd neglected her duty to check on him last night; the last thing she wanted was to wake him up before she'd found some way to redeem herself.

Turning on her heel, she moved as quietly as she could to the stairs and down them. Her first stop was the kitchen. She put coffee on, then surveyed the contents of the fridge. Though she knew every single item in it, it was fun to look at all those goodies and pretend she might have something greasy and bad for her like bacon and eggs. Of course, she didn't. She settled for the less satisfying but healthy grapefruit and cereal. Then she poured herself a cup of coffee and sipped it as she peered out the window into Lucern's backyard. It was a large, neat, tidy lawn surrounded by trees, obviously professionally kept. Just as the house was.

Lucern's home bespoke wealth and class, both inside and out. It was large and filled with antiques, but outside was the true treat. The house was set on a good-sized property surrounded by trees and grass, all well kept and set up to disguise the fact that the home sat on the edge of a huge metropolis. It was gorgeous and restful, and Kate enjoyed it as she drank her coffee.

Pouring herself another cup, she wandered out of the kitchen and strolled up the hall, her mind searching for some plot to keep her in the house for at least another night. She really had to convince Lucern to do at least one of the interviews. Kate suspected he would never agree to do the book-signing tour and she had already let go of that idea, but surely he could be persuaded to do a couple of interviews. Possibly over the phone or via the Internet? A couple of her other authors had done it via e-mail. The interviewer sent an e-mail with the questions, the author answered by e-mail. Or there were the various messenger services; she'd heard of authors doing interviews that way as well. Geez, surely that wouldn't be such a big deal? Lucern wouldn't even have to leave his house.

She was about to turn into the living room with her

coffee when she spotted the box on the hall table. Kate recognized it at once. She'd packed the damned thing full of fan letters and sent it herself. Changing direction, she continued up the hall to the table and glared down at the box. She'd sent it three months ago! Three months! And he hadn't even bothered to open the damned thing, let alone answer any of the letters it held.

"Damned man," she muttered. "Ungrateful, stupid . . . *wonderful* man." The last was said with a dawning smile as she recognized her excuse for staying another night. "Oh," she breathed. "God bless your stupid hide and rude ways."

Salsa music. That was the first thing Lucern heard upon awaking. He recognized the tune; it was a hit at the moment. A brief image flashed in his head of a thin, handsome Latin man dancing around on a stage in dark clothes.

The music made it easy for him to find Kate. He merely followed the sound to his living room, where he paused in the doorway to gape at the shambles the room had become while he slept. The room that had been neat and tidy when he went to bed was now awash in paper. Every available surface had open letters and envelopes piled on it. Kate C. Leever boogied around a box in the center of the mess, pulling letters out, opening them, and gyrating to one pile or another to add the letter to it before boogying back for another.

"You poked!" he roared.

Kate, who had been doing some sort of bump and grind—a rather sexy bump and grind, to be honest—

52

with the half-empty box, gave a squeak of alarm. She whirled toward the door, upsetting the box and sending it to the floor.

"Now look what you made me do!" she cried, flushing with embarrassment. She bent to gather up the box and its contents.

"You poked," Lucern repeated. Moving forward, he towered over her as she scooped up the escaped envelopes.

"I . . ." She peered up at him guiltily, then irritation took over her expression. Standing, she glared back. "I hardly needed to poke. The box was right there on the hall table. I noticed it in passing."

"I am not sure, but I believe it is illegal to open someone else's mail. Is it not a federal offense?"

"I'm quite sure that doesn't apply when it's mail you sent yourself—and I *did* send this box. Three months ago!" she added grimly.

"But you did not write the letters inside it."

Kate scowled, then turned her attention to throwing the unopened envelopes back in the box. She explained, "I saw that you hadn't even opened it yet, and thought perhaps I could help. It was obvious you were overwhelmed by the number of letters."

"Ha! I had no idea of the number of letters. I hadn't opened it."

"No, you hadn't," she conceded after a moment. Then she asked, "What is it with you and mail? I've never met anyone who left mail lying about for months like this. It's no wonder you were so slow to answer my letters."

Before he could respond, she turned and added,

"And how could you ignore these letters like you did?" She waved at the mini-towers built around the room. "These are your readers, your fans! Without them, you're nothing. They pay good money for your books, and more good money to tell you they enjoyed them. Your books wouldn't be published without readers to read them. How can you just ignore them like this? They took the time and trouble to write you. They say wonderful things about you, your books, your writing! Didn't you ever admire someone's work or enjoy it so much you wanted to tell them of your appreciation? You should be grateful they've taken the trouble to do so!"

Lucern stared at her with surprise. She was quite impassioned, her face flushed, her chest heaving. And what a nice chest it was, he noted. She had a nice figure altogether, even in the comfortable jeans and T-shirt she'd chosen to wear today.

All of which was interesting to note, but not very useful at the moment. He reprimanded himself and took a moment to clear his throat before trying to speak. The problem was, he couldn't recall what she'd said or what he should say in response.

"Ha!" There was triumph on her face. "You have no answer to that one, do you? Because it's true. You have been terribly lax in tending to this matter, and I've decided—out of the goodness of my heart—to help you. You needn't thank me," she added in a rather self-righteous tone. Then she grabbed and opened another letter.

Lucern found a grin pulling at his lips as he watched her. He didn't have to be able to read her mind to know that this was not out of the goodness of her heart, but an attempt to remain in his home long enough to convince him to do some of her publicity stuff. He decided—out of the goodness of *his* heart—to let her stay long enough to help him with the letters. He hadn't intended to answer them. He didn't know any of these people and it was a burdensome task, but now . . . Well, her tirade had actually reached him. To some degree.

"Very well. You may help me with the letters," he announced.

Kate shook her head at Lucern Argeneau's magnanimity. "Well! How grand of you to allow me to . . ." She paused. Her sneering words were a wasted effort; Lucern had left the room. Damned man! He was the most frustrating, irritating . . . And what was with his proper speech all the time? The man had antique phrasing and a slight accent that she couldn't quite place. Both of which were beginning to annoy her.

She was just turning back to the box to continue sorting the letters into categories when a series of loud chimes rang through the house. Recognizing it to be the doorbell, she hesitated, then dropped the letters and went to answer. She opened the front door to find a uniformed man on the other side, a cooler stamped "A.B.B." in hand.

"Hi." He stopped chewing the gum in his mouth long enough to grin at her, showing off a nice set of white teeth. "You must be Luc's editor."

Kate lifted her eyebrows. "Er, yes. Kate. Kate C. Leever."

The man took the hand she held out and squeezed it warmly. "Aunt Maggie was right. You're a cutey."

55

"Aunt Maggie?" Kate asked in confusion.

"Luc's mom and my aunt. Marguerite," he added when she continued to look confused, but it didn't help Kate much. The only people she'd met since arriving were the pair who had been leaving when she got out of the taxi, and the woman certainly hadn't been old enough to be Luc's—er, Lucern's—mother. Kate shrugged that concern aside as the other connotations of what he'd said sank in. "You're Lucern's cousin?"

"Yes, ma'am. Our dads are brothers." He grinned, making it hard for her to see a resemblance. Oh, this man was tallish and had dark hair like Lucern, but Luc didn't smile, and this young man hadn't stopped smiling since she'd opened the door. It was hard to believe they were related. "I'm quite a bit younger though."

"You are?" she asked doubtfully. She would have placed both men around the same age.

"Oh, yes." He grinned. "I'm centuries younger than Lucern."

"Thomas."

Kate glanced over her shoulder. Lucern was coming up the hall, a scowl on his face as he glanced from her to his cousin. She sighed inwardly at his obvious displeasure. Apparently, he didn't like her answering his door. Geez, the guy was such a pain. Why couldn't Thomas here have written the vampire novels? He would have been much easier to deal with, she was sure.

"Here you are, Cousin." Thomas didn't seem surprised or disturbed by Lucern's expression. He held out the cooler. "Bastien said to get this here pronto. That you were seriously lacking and in need," he added with a grin and a wink.

"Thank you."

Lucern actually smiled at his cousin, Kate noted with surprise. And his face didn't crack and fall off.

"I'll return directly," Lucern added. As he turned toward the stairs he warned, "Try not to bite my guest. She can be . . . provoking."

Kate scowled at her host's retreating back, then smiled reluctantly at Thomas's chuckle. She turned with a wry smile and asked, "Has he always been this irritable, or is it just me?"

"Just you," Thomas said. At her crestfallen expression, he started to laugh. Then he took pity on her and told the truth. "Nah. It isn't you. Lucern is kind of surly. Has been for centuries. Although he seems to be in a good mood today. You must be having a good influence on him."

"This is a good mood?" Kate asked with disbelief. Thomas just laughed again.

"Here you are," Lucern called. He jogged down the steps and handed his cousin's cooler back to him. "Give Bastien my thanks."

"Will do." Then Thomas nodded, gave Kate another wink, and turned to walk off the porch.

Kate glanced at the driveway and the truck parked in it. "A.B.B. Deliveries" was stamped on the side, the same as the cooler, she noted. Lucern maneuvered her out of the way and closed the door.

"What . . . ?" she began curiously, but Lucern saved her from proving just how rude and nosy she could be. He turned away and started back up the hall before she could ask the questions trembling on her lips.

*　　*　　*

57

"I thought that, as there are so many letters—too many to answer individually, really—we could divide them into categories and come up with a sort of form letter for each. Then you could just add a line to each response to make it more personal."

Lucern grunted and took another sip of the coffee Kate had made while making lunch. Well, it had been her lunch, his breakfast. Although, if he counted the bag of blood he'd sucked down while stacking the rest Thomas had delivered in the small refrigerator in his office, he supposed the meal could count as his lunch, too. They had since moved to the living room, and he was seated on the couch while she explained her plans for his letters.

"I'll take that to mean you think my plan is brilliant and agree to cooperate," Kate said in response to his grunt. Because it seemed to annoy her, and because he liked the way she flushed when she was annoyed, Lucern grunted again.

As he expected, her cheeks pinkened with blood and her eyes sparked with anger, and Lucern decided that Kate C. Leever was a pretty little thing when angry. He enjoyed looking at her.

And despite her unhappiness with him, the irritation on her face suddenly eased and she commented, "You have more color today. I guess there was no lasting damage from that head wound after all."

"I told you I was fine," Luc said.

"Yes, you did," she agreed. Then she looked uncomfortable and said, "I'm sorry I didn't check on you after that first time. I intended to, but I didn't hear the alarm go off again. I must have turned it off in my sleep or something."

Lucern waved the apology away. He had turned the alarm off himself, so she had nothing to apologize for. And he didn't think she'd appreciate knowing that he'd crept into her room while she was sleeping. She most definitely wouldn't want to know that after finishing the task, he'd found himself standing at the side of the bed just watching her sleep for a while, staring with fascination at her innocent expression in sleep, watching the rise and fall of the bunnies on her flannel nightgown as she breathed. How he'd wanted to pull the top of that oh-so-proper nightgown away from her throat to see the pulse beating there. No, she definitely wouldn't want to know all that, so he kept it to himself and sipped his coffee again.

The drink was bitter, but an oddly tasty brew. Lucern couldn't think why he'd avoided it all these years. True, he'd been warned that the stimulant in coffee would hit his body twice as hard as a human's, but he really hadn't noticed any effects yet. Of course, he'd only had a couple sips so far. Perhaps he shouldn't risk any more. He set the cup down.

"So, what are we doing?" he asked abruptly, to get Kate off the topic of not waking up to check on him last night.

"Well, I've been dividing the letters into categories. A lot of them have similar themes or questions, such as requests as to whether you'll write Lucern's or Bastien's story next," she explained. "So I've been putting all those asking that question in one pile. That way, you can write a form letter for each pile, reducing the letters you write to twenty or so rather than hundreds and hundreds."

"Of course, it would be nice if you read each letter and wrote a line or two to personalize your response," she added, sounding tentative.

Lucern supposed she thought that the idea of all that work would annoy him. Which it did. He couldn't help but grumble, "I did not suffer these difficulties with my other books."

"Other books?" She blinked in confusion, then said, "Oh. You mean your historical texts. Well, that was different. Those were nonfiction. Most of them are used in universities and such. Students rarely write fan letters."

Lucern grimaced and gulped down another mouthful of coffee. It helped stop him from telling her that his novels were nonfiction as well, and that they were just peddled as vampire romance.

"Anyway, I think we have enough categories to make a start. I can tell you what each category is, and you can compose a sort of general response to each while I continue to sort the rest of the letters," she suggested.

Nodding his acquiescence, Lucern crossed his arms and waited.

"Wouldn't you like to get a pen and paper or something?" she asked after a moment. "So you don't forget any of them? There are at least twenty categories and—"

"I have an excellent memory," Lucern announced. "Proceed."

Kate turned in a slow circle, apparently trying to decide where to start. "Dear God, he sounds like that bald guy in *The King and I*," he heard her mutter.

Lucern knew he wasn't supposed to hear that, but he had spectacular hearing. He quite enjoyed her exasperation, so he added to it by commenting, "You mean Yul Brynner."

She jerked around to eye him with alarm, and he nodded. "He played the king of Siam, and did an excellent job of it."

Kate hesitated; then, apparently deciding that he wasn't angry, she relaxed a bit and even managed a smile. "It's one of my favorite movies."

"Oh, did they make a movie of it?" he asked with interest. "I saw it live on stage on opening night."

When she appeared rather doubtful, he realized that admitting to seeing the Rodgers and Hammerstein Broadway show—which had premiered in 1951, if he wasn't mistaken—was rather dating himself. As he looked to be in his mid-thirties, it was no wonder she appeared taken aback. Clearing his throat, he added, "The revival of course. It hit Broadway in 1977, I believe."

Her eyebrows rose. "You must have been all of ... what? Seven? Eight?"

Unwilling to lie, Lucern merely grunted. He added, "I have an excellent memory."

"Yes. Of course you do." Kate sighed and picked up a letter. She read aloud, " 'Dear Mr. Argeneau. I read and adored Love Bites, volumes one and two. But the first was my favorite. You truly have a talent! The medieval feel to that novel was so gritty and realistic that I could almost believe you were there.' " Kate paused and glanced up. "All the letters in this stack are along that line, praising you for the realism of your writing and the fact that it reads as if you were actually there."

When Lucern merely nodded, she frowned. "Well?"

"Well, what?" he asked with surprise. "That reader is right."

"That reader is right?" She gaped at him. "That's what you're going to write? 'Dear reader, You're right?' "

Lucern shrugged mildly, wondering why she was raising her voice. The reader *was right*. His books did read as if he'd been there in medieval times. Because he had been. Not during the precise time period when his parents met, but not long afterward—and in those days, change was slow enough that little had differed.

He watched his editor slam the letter back on the pile and move on to another. She muttered the whole time about him being an arrogant jerk, and added other uncomplimentary descriptions. "Insensitive" and "lacking in social skills" were just two. All of which Lucern knew he wasn't supposed to hear.

He wasn't offended. He was six hundred years old. A man gained some self-confidence in that time. Lucern supposed that to most people he *would* seem arrogant, possibly even a jerk. Insensitive certainly, and he knew his social skills were somewhat rusty. Etienne and Bastien had always been better at this social stuff. Yet, after years of living as a reclusive author, he was terribly lacking and knew it.

Still, he couldn't see any good reason to sharpen those social skills. He was at that stage in life where impressing someone seemed like a load of bother.

He'd taken a waitress for dinner once who'd explained the way he felt rather nicely. She'd said, "You can go along, working your shift and everything's fine. Most of the customers are pretty good, though there might be the occasional bad one. But sometimes you have that night where you get a real nasty customer, or even two or three in a row, and they bring you down, make you tired and miserable, feeling like the whole human race sucks. Then a baby might coo and smile at you, or another customer will say "Rough night?" with a sympathetic smile. Then your mood picks up and you'll realize maybe people aren't so bad."

Well, Lucern had suffered a couple of bad decades, and he was feeling tired and depressed and as if the whole human race rather sucked. He didn't have the energy or desire to put up with people. He just wanted to be left alone. That was why he'd started writing—a solitary pursuit that kept him busy and took him into much more pleasant worlds.

He knew that all it would take was someone to smile and say "rough decade?" to change that. Someone like Kate. As much as he'd resisted having to deal with her, he'd begun to enjoy her company. She'd even made him smile several times.

Realizing the path his thoughts were taking, and that they were rather warmer than he was comfortable feeling for his unwanted house guest, he drew himself up short and began to scowl. Dear God, what had he been thinking? Kate C. Leever was a stubborn, annoying woman who had done nothing but bring chaos to an orderly existence. He—

" 'Dear Mr Argeneau,' " she read grimly, drawing Lucern out of his thoughts. " 'I've read your vampire novels and enjoyed them immensely. I have always been fascinated with vampirism and read everything on the subject voraciously. I just know that there really is such a thing, and suspect you yourself really are one. I would love to be one. Would you please turn me into a vampire, too?' " Kate rolled her eyes and stopped reading, glancing at him. "What would you say to *her*?"

"No," he said firmly.

Kate threw the letter down with a snort. "Why does that answer not surprise me? Although I suppose it would be ridiculous to try to explain to someone of that ilk that you really aren't a vampire, that there truly is no such thing, so you couldn't possibly 'change' her." She laughed and moved on to the next pile. Looking at the first few letters there, she added, "It would be kinder just to tell her to go to her local psychologist to see if he couldn't help her with her reality problem."

Lucern felt his lips twitch, but he didn't say anything, merely waited as Kate settled on the next letter.

" 'Dear Mr. Argeneau,' " she began. " 'I haven't read Love Bites, One, but I will, I guarantee it. I just finished Love Bites, Two, and thought it was wonderful. Etienne was so sweet and funny and sexy that I fell in love with him even as Rachel did. He's my dream man.' " Kate paused and glanced up expectantly. "What would you say to those letters?"

That was easy enough. "Etienne is taken."

His editor threw her hands up in the air. "This isn't a joke, Lucern! You can't just—" She paused as the doorbell chimed, then turned away with a sigh as Lucern reluctantly stood to answer it. He already knew who it would be. Thomas had delivered the blood, which left

64

the only other company he ever got: his family. And since Etienne and Rachel were busy with wedding preparations, and Bastien, Lissianna and Gregory would all be at work at this hour, the only person it could be was his . . .

"Mother." His greeting was less than enthusiastic as he opened the door to find Marguerite Argeneau standing there. He really had no desire to have his mother and Kate Leever in the same room; it would definitely give the older woman ideas. And since he already suspected she tended in those ideas' direction, he didn't think it was good to encourage her. But what could he do? She was his mother.

"Luc, darling." Marguerite kissed him on both cheeks, then pushed past him into the house. "Are you alone, dear? I thought I'd drop in for a spot of tea." She didn't wait for his answer, but followed her maternal instincts to the door of the living room and smiled brightly when she spotted Kate. "Well, it looks like I'm just in time. No doubt you two could use a break, too."

Lucern closed his front door with a resigned sigh, and his mother sailed fearlessly into his cluttered living room. The woman never simply stopped by for tea. She always had a purpose. And Luc very much feared he wasn't going to like her purpose in stopping by today. He just hoped to God she knew better than to try any of her matchmaking nonsense on him and Kate.

Chapter Four

"Why, you could be Luc's date!"

"Er . . ." Kate cast a frantic glance Lucern's way at his mother's suggestion, only to find him sitting with eyes closed, a pained expression on his face. She suspected he was begging for the floor to open up and swallow him whole, or even to swallow him in pieces, so long as it swallowed him. It almost made Kate feel better. It was nice to know that she wasn't the only one with parents who managed to humiliate her at every opportunity.

Still, Marguerite was really something else. Kate had spent the better part of the half hour since the woman's arrival merely gaping at her. This exotic and beautiful creature was Lucern's mother? Oh, certainly, the resemblance was there. And he was equal to her in looks, but Marguerite Argeneau didn't look a day over thirty herself. How could she possibly be Lucern's—or Luc, as everyone seemed to call him—mom?

"Good genes, dear," had been the woman's answer when Kate had commented.

Kate had sighed miserably, wondering why such genes couldn't run in her family, too. After that, she'd merely stared at the woman, nodding absently at everything said, while trying to spot signs of a face lift. She obviously should have been paying more attention to what Marguerite was burbling on about. Lucern's brother's wedding had been the topic of conversation. Kate wasn't quite sure how that had led to the last comment she had heard.

"Date?" she repeated blankly.

"Yes, dear. For the wedding."

"Mother." Lucern's voice was a warning growl, and Kate peered over to see that his eyes were open and sharply focused on his mother.

"Well, Luc darling. You can hardly leave the poor girl here alone tomorrow night while you attend." Marguerite laughed, apparently oblivious to her son's fury.

"Kate has to return to New York," Lucern said firmly. "She won't be here tomorrow ni—"

"That sounds like fun!" Kate blurted. Lucern fell silent and aimed his gimlet eye at her, but she ignored him. There was no way she was leaving without first gaining his agreement to at least an interview with one of the newspapers clamoring to speak to him. And falling in with Marguerite's suggestion meant that not only could he not force her on a plane back to New York, but by the time the wedding party was over, it would be too late for Kate to fly home the next night as well. Which gave her until Sunday to work on the man. That thought made her beam happily, and she silently thanked Lucern's mother.

The only thing that worried her was that Marguerite Argeneau was looking rather pleased in return. Kate had the sudden anxious feeling that she'd stepped neatly into a trap. She hoped to God that the woman didn't have any matchmaking ideas about her and Lucern. Surely Marguerite realized what a cantankerous lout her son was and that he wasn't Kate's type at all!

"Well, wonderful!" the woman said. Ignoring her son's scowl, Marguerite smiled like the cat who got the cream, then asked, "Do you have something to wear to the wedding, dear?"

"Oh." Kate's smile faltered. She'd packed something for every possible occasion except a wedding. There'd been no way to see *that* coming, and Kate didn't think the slinky black dress she'd brought to cover the possibility of an evening out would work.

"Ah-ha!" Lucern was now the one looking pleased. "She hasn't anything to wear, Mother. She can't—"

"A quick trip to my modiste, I think," Marguerite cut him off. Then she confided to Kate, "She always has something for just such an emergency. And a visit with my hairdresser will work magic on your hair, and we'll be set."

Kate felt herself relax, and could have hugged the woman. Marguerite was wonderful. Much too good to have a son like Lucern. The woman was clever, charming and a pleasure to be around. Unlike a certain surly man. Kate's gaze slid to Lucern, and she almost grinned at the misery on his face. She supposed she should feel guilty for forcing herself into his home and staying there, but she didn't. He was in serious need of assistance. He was terribly lacking in social skills and obviously spent way too much time alone. She was good for him—she was sure of it.

"Well, now that it's all settled, I'll be off." Marguerite was quickly on her feet and heading out of the kitchen—so quickly that Kate nearly got whiplash watching.

Getting up, she hurried after the woman. "Thank you so much, Mrs. Argeneau," she called as she jogged down the hall in pursuit.

Lucern's mother didn't just look young, she was as spry as could be for the mother of a man who had to be at least thirty-five. How old did that make her? Kate wondered. At least fifty-three. Impossible, she thought, but kept the thought to herself and merely added, "I really appreciate your generous offer to help me shop and—"

"Nonsense, dear. I'm grateful to you for being here to accompany Luc." Marguerite paused and allowed Kate to catch up. "Why, you should have seen the poor man at his *sister's* wedding. I've never seen Luc run so fast or hide so much. It's the ladies, you know. They tend to chase after him."

Kate's eyebrows flew up in patent disbelief at that.

A bubble of laughter burst from Marguerite. "Hard to believe when Luc is so curmudgeonly, isn't it? But I think it's the hunt that attracts them. He makes it obvious he isn't interested, and they react like hounds after a fox. With you there to act as his escort, he'll be able to relax and enjoy the celebration this time. And once he realizes that, he'll be grateful for your presence, too."

Kate didn't bother to hide her doubt that Lucern Argeneau could ever be grateful for anything. The man was more than curmudgeonly in her opinion.

"He may seem crusty on the outside, dear," Marguerite said solemnly, obviously reading her thoughts. "But he's rather like a toasted marshmallow, soft and mushy in the center. Very few people ever see that center, though." Leaving Kate to consider that, the older woman continued on to the door and opened it. "I shall pick you up after lunch. One o'clock. If that's all right with you?"

"Yes. But will that leave time to get everything done?" Kate asked with concern. In her experience, weddings were usually around two or three o'clock in the afternoon.

Marguerite Argeneau looked calm. "Oh, scads of time, dear. The wedding isn't until seven p.m."

"Isn't that rather late?" Kate asked with surprise.

"Late weddings are all the rage today. I hear Julia Roberts married her cameraman after midnight."

"Really? I hadn't heard that," Kate said faintly.

"Oh yes. She's started a trend. Till tomorrow then," Marguerite finished gaily. The woman then closed the door behind herself, leaving Kate standing in the hallway feeling rather as if she'd just survived a tornado.

Kate stood there for several minutes, just staring at the door, her mind whirring through everything she would need to do to be ready for this wedding, before the door to the kitchen opened and Lucern stalked out.

"I'll be in my office." His voice was short, his expression forbidding as he passed her on the way to the stairs.

Kate—always a smart girl when it came to matters of self-preservation—kept her mouth shut and merely watched him disappear up the stairs. He was angry, of course. Which was to be expected, but she hoped it would pass.

A door slammed upstairs. Hard.

Well, perhaps he wouldn't get over it tonight, but he would by tomorrow. She hoped. With a little help, maybe. She turned and peered at the mess in the living room. There was no way she was going to be able to get him to work on those letters tonight. Which she supposed was a good thing. She was beginning to fear that any letters he wrote were more likely to offend and scare readers than please them. She'd be doing him a big favor by composing the form letters herself and just having him sign them.

Kate grimaced at the idea. It meant a lot of work for her, and the readers were hardly likely to be all that happy. They'd certainly be happier with her meddling, however, than with receiving a letter that read:

Dear Reader.
  No.
Sincerely,
Lucern Argeneau

Oddly enough, Kate found herself chuckling at the idea. He really was rather amusing in some ways, this author of hers. The problem was, he didn't mean to be.

Heaving a sigh, she turned into the living room to start to work.

* * *

71

Lucern grabbed a bag of blood from the small office refrigerator where he'd placed it earlier, then paced his office like a caged tiger. He did so for more than an hour before working off enough energy so that he could relax sufficiently to sit. He didn't know if it was his anger or the caffeine that had got him so wound up. And he didn't care.

Groaning, he leaned back in his desk chair and rubbed his face with his hands. His mother had just cursed him to two more nights of Kate Leever's presence. And Kate hadn't helped matters with her quick agreement. The woman was like lichen. Like muck you couldn't scrape off the bottom of your shoe. Like—well, none of the things popping to his mind were very attractive, and, as annoying as Kate Leever could be, she was also attractive, so Lucern gave up his analogies. He tried to be fair about such things whenever possible.

Letting his hands drop away from his face, he turned to consider the computer on his desk. He wanted to avoid Kate for a bit. He was still cranky enough that he was likely to hurt her feelings were he around her, and he didn't wish to hurt her—

"Well, hell! Now you're worried about her feelings?" he said to himself. This wouldn't do at all. He tried to be firm with his unruly sentiments and lectured, "The woman is your editor. She will use manipulation, clever ruses and any weapon necessary to get what she wants from you. Do not start getting all soft and sentimental about her. You don't want her here. You want to be left alone to work in peace."

The problem was, he didn't really have anything to work on. He hadn't started anything new since finishing

Etienne and Rachel's story—which had been in print for a month now. And Lucern didn't have a clue what to work on next. He knew that Kate and Roundhouse Publishing wanted another vampire romance, but Bastien wasn't showing signs of obliging his brother by falling in love any time soon.

Well, Lucern decided with a shrug, it wasn't as if he needed the money. His investments over the years had always done well. He could relax if he wanted. Roundhouse would just have to wait until he came up with something.

His gaze fell on the video game on the corner of his desk—*Blood Lust II*. The game was Etienne's newest creation. Part I had sold out several times and won countless awards. Its success wasn't a great surprise to Lucern; the game was fun and action-packed, with awesome graphics, lots of villains to slay, lots of puzzles to solve and a great story line. Lucern wasn't the only one in the family who could write a story. Blood Lust II was expected to do even better when it was released.

Grinning, he popped the seal on the package and pulled out the game CD. He had played the first couple of levels of the prototype before the game was even finished, and he and Bastien had got the first two full copies hot off the press. It paid to be brothers of the creator.

Lucern slipped the game into his computer and prepared to enjoy himself. He would work off some of his anger by slaughtering bad guys. And he'd also avoid Kate for a while. He'd found the perfect solution.

*   *   *

73

LYNSAY SANDS

He had played for several hours and was deep into the game when he heard the knock at the door. At his distracted "What?" the door opened and Kate stepped into the room carrying a tray.

"I thought you might be hungry."

Her tentative words, along with the smell of food, drew Lucern's attention away from the game. He sniffed with interest, thinking he could manage some at that moment. He, like the rest of his family, ate food as well as ingested blood. If they didn't, they'd all be skinny wraiths.

"What is it?" he asked curiously.

"Well, I knew I was going to be busy—I've been working on the letters," she informed him. "So, after your mother left and you went upstairs, I threw the roast we picked up into the oven with some potatoes. That way it would cook while I worked. You said you like rare everything. I hope that includes roast, because this roast is pretty rare."

"Perfect." Lucern took the tray and set it on his desk, noting that there were two plates of food and two glasses of what looked to be wine and two glasses of water as well. She'd covered all the bases.

He was just relaxing when she began to drag a chair around the desk to join him and said, "I was hoping we could discuss—"

She was about to bring up the publicity issue again. Lucern immediately felt himself begin to tense; then Kate's gaze landed on the computer screen.

"That looks like Blood Lust."

"Blood Lust Two," he corrected.

"You're kidding. Really? It isn't supposed to be out until Monday. I have it on order."

"I know the creator," Lucern admitted reluctantly. "I got an early copy."

"No way. You lucky dog! Is it as good as the first?"

"Better." Lucern began to relax again as she continued staring avidly at the frozen screen. He recognized a fellow gamer when he saw one. Any talk of publicity had probably just bit the dust for the night.

He glanced at the screen and saw that his character had died while he'd been distracted. The game was waiting for him to decide what to do next. His options were to start over, or quit the game. He considered the matter briefly, then asked, "Do you want to play? You can play doubles on it."

"Really?" She looked terribly excited. "Yes, please. I love Blood Lust, and I've been waiting forever for Two to come out." She dragged her chair even closer. "This is great."

Lucern smiled to himself and started the game over. He'd say one thing for her: Kate C. Leever had good taste. She liked his books, and she liked Etienne's game.

She also proved to be one hell of a game player. The dinner she had made sat forgotten on the desk as they worked through the levels he'd already run through, then continued on to the next levels, working together to defeat the villains and save the damsel in distress. Every time they succeeded at accessing another level, Kate reacted with the excitement of a child and they did a high five or a little victory dance at the desk while they waited for the next level to load.

They played for hours, until the food was a shriveled

and congealed mess, until their necks and hands ached, and until Kate began nodding off in her seat. When Lucern reluctantly suggested it might be best if she went to bed, she agreed with equal reluctance that she should or she wouldn't be able to get up for the shopping trip with his mother.

Oddly enough, Lucern missed her once she was gone. He continued on through another level of the game, but it wasn't the same without her there to share the glee at succeeding. There were no high fives or little victory dances, and he was troubled to find he missed those, too. Even more troubling was the fact that for the first time in years, Lucern felt lonely.

Despite her late night, Kate was up and ready at one o'clock. She stood anxiously waiting by the front door watching for Mrs. Argeneau. When a limo pulled into the driveway, she hurried outside and started down the porch stairs, then paused and turned back uncertainly toward the door. She had unbolted it to leave and didn't have a clue what to do about bolting it again. Dare she leave it unlocked? Or should she wake up Lucern and have him bolt it?

"It's all right, Kate. Don't worry about the door," Marguerite unrolled the back window to call out. "Come along, we've lots to do."

Shrugging inwardly, Kate turned and walked over to the limo. The driver was out to open the door for her by the time she reached it, and Kate murmured a thank-you as she slipped inside; then she did a double take at the sight of Lucern's mother. The woman was bundled up as if they were in the midst of a winter storm.

She had on a long-sleeved blouse, gloves and slacks, then a scarf over her head and covering the bottom half of her face. Over-large sunglasses covered most of the rest. The only patch of skin showing was her nose, and that was slathered with a white cream Kate guessed to be sunblock.

"Don't tell me. You're allergic to the sun like Lucern?" Kate guessed.

Marguerite's mouth twisted in wry amusement. "Where do you think he got it?"

Kate gave a laugh and relaxed back in the limo, prepared for a day of both frantic shopping and pampering. And that was exactly what she got: a frantic rush to choose the perfect dress and see it tailored to fit her, then a couple of hours of delicious pampering at the spa where Marguerite Argeneau's hair stylist worked. She enjoyed herself immensely.

Luc didn't sleep well. He went to bed out of sheer boredom not long after Kate left, but he couldn't find rest. The woman hadn't just invaded his home, she'd made her way into his dreams, too. That fact was enough to make him terribly grumpy on awakening, and it was a surly Lucern who stumbled downstairs Saturday afternoon. He became even more surly when a quick search of the house showed that Kate hadn't yet returned from her shopping sojourn.

Grumbling under his breath, he made his way to the kitchen and—out of habit—opened the refrigerator door looking for blood. It wasn't until he had the door open that he recalled sticking his supply in the tiny fridge in his office, to keep it out of Kate's sight. He

considered going back upstairs to fetch a bag, but
didn't really feel like it. He didn't really feel like normal
food either despite the fact that he and Kate had sac-
rificed supper the night before for Blood Lust II. And
he knew he would be eating a lot of rich food at the
wedding celebration, so it was better to put off eating
now.

Deciding he'd grab a bag of blood later before leaving for the wedding, Lucern wandered aimlessly out of
the kitchen and moved along the hall to the living
room. He immediately grimaced. Kate had finished
sorting the letters into categories, and there were several form letters awaiting his signature.

Curious, Lucern sat on the couch and began to read
through them. They were all very nice, chatty letters
that sounded gracious and charming and not at all like
him. Kate was a good writer, too. She'd done a wonderful job, and Lucern supposed he'd have to thank
her. He also supposed he should hire an assistant to
manage such tasks in the future. Unfortunately, he
knew he wouldn't. The idea of a stranger in his home,
pawing through his things was not a happy one. That
was the reason he still hadn't replaced his housekeeper,
Mrs. Johnson. The woman had died in her sleep in
1995. Which was eight years ago, he realized with surprise.

Since, Lucern had hired a service to clean his home
once a week, and he usually had his meals out or ordered them from a gourmet restaurant down the street.
He'd intended to do that only until he found a replace-
ment for the unfortunate Mrs. Johnson, which he'd
never gotten around to. He'd think about it and all the
trouble it meant, then would decide against it. Why go

to all that time and effort only to have whomever he hired drop dead on him after ten or twenty years as both Mrs. Johnson and Edwin had done?

He muttered under his breath at the thought. Humans were so unreliable that way. They were forever dropping dead on you just when you had them trained.

He was pondering that annoying little habit of mankind when the front door of the house slammed. Kate was back from her shopping excursion. He ran his hands through his hair, brushed down his T-shirt and tried to look presentable. He sat up, peering expectantly toward the living room door . . . and was just in time to catch a glimpse of Kate flying upstairs. At least he thought it was Kate. All he'd really seen was a go-dawful bundle of shopping bags with various designer names on them, and feet.

Oh, yes. She'd been shopping. He slumped back on the couch with disgust. She hadn't even noticed him. Women!

A cacophony of sounds followed from upstairs—the slamming of the guest room door, then all sorts of unidentifiable banging and bumping. It sounded as if the woman was jumping around and throwing things willy-nilly.

It went on long enough that Lucern became concerned. Then there was a sudden and utter silence. Standing, he walked into the hallway and peered anxiously up the stairs. A door opened and closed; then he heard the clicking of high-heeled shoes on the hardwood hall floor, and Kate appeared at the top of the steps.

She was a sight. A vision. Her golden hair was piled

on top of her head with little ringlets dropping down to frame her pretty, flushed face. The gown she wore was a deep emerald green. It had a long skirt, a crepe neck, and was made of a soft-looking material that had a slight sheen as it draped gracefully over the contours and curves of her body. She was glorious. An angel. The most beautiful woman Lucern had seen in his life, and that was saying something. He was tongue-tied with amazement. He simply watched in awe as she descended the steps.

She was only halfway down when she spotted him. She immediately paused, blinked, then scowled. "You aren't ready!"

It was Lucern's turn to blink. His angel was bellowing. She was also frantic. The serene vision was gone.

"Lucern!" She glared at him with disbelief. "The wedding is at seven o'clock! It's six-fifteen now. We have to leave. You haven't even showered or anything! What have you been doing all this time?" She covered her lower face with horror. "We'll be late! I hate being late to weddings. Everyone will be seated in the pews, and they'll all stare and—"

"Okay!" Lucern held up his hands, trying to soothe her as he started up the stairs. "It's okay. I'm fast. I'll be ready. Just give me ten minutes. We won't be late," he assured her as he moved warily past her. "Really. I promise."

Kate watched with exasperation as Lucern disappeared up the stairs. Once he was out of sight, her shoulders drooped unhappily. After all her efforts, he hadn't even commented on how she looked.

Disappointed, she continued downstairs and went

into the living room to wait. She was all prepared to tap a hole in the floor with impatience. She didn't get the chance. Ten minutes after leaving her on the steps, Lucern came back downstairs all set to go. His hair was still damp from the shower and slicked back, and a tailored designer suit hung elegantly off his broad shoulders.

Ten minutes, Kate thought with disgust. Ten minutes, and he looked fabulous. It had taken her all day to put herself together, and it had taken him ten minutes! She glared at him as she joined him in the hall.

"See? I told you I'd be fast," Lucern said soothingly as he opened the front door. "We won't be late. We'll be right on time."

Still irritated that he'd been so quick, Kate merely made a face and led the way outside.

Lucern opened the passenger door of his BMW in a rather courtly manner she appreciated, then commented, "You look lovely." He closed the door before she could respond, but Kate smiled widely as she watched him walk around the car to the driver's side. Her mood was beginning to lift again. Kate generally disliked weddings, and she would definitely be uncomfortable at being called "Luc's date," but maybe tonight wouldn't be so bad.

Chapter Five

It was awful. Well, not entirely, Lucern admitted to himself. The wedding ceremony itself was beautiful. And much to his surprise, his stubborn, pesky editor got all teary-eyed as Etienne and Rachel exchanged their vows. She explained herself when he handed her the handkerchief he'd placed in his breast pocket with such care by saying, "They seem so happy. They're obviously deeply in love."

Lucern merely grunted and hoped the ceremony wouldn't be as long as Lissianna's had been last year. He only had the one hanky.

Fortunately, Rachel's minister wasn't as long-winded as the Hewitt family's minister had been. Still, Lucern practically ran Kate out of the church the moment it was done. Or tried to. Their escape was stalled by the bottleneck that formed at the exit as each and every single guest paused to wish Etienne and Rachel well. The couple had exited the church first, as per the custom, and were now standing atop the church steps, speaking to everyone as they left.

Of course, Kate would insist on congratulating them and wishing them well, too, which Lucern thought was ridiculous. She didn't even know them! But the woman ignored his attempts to urge her down the stairs, and stopped to wish the couple happiness.

Rachel and Etienne weren't surprised Kate was at the wedding, of course. The family grapevine was as healthy as ever. And much to Lucern's irritation, Rachel was one of those social people who liked everyone and liked to talk. Etienne was hampered with the same affliction, so they couldn't just say thank-you and let Kate go. No. They had to actually *speak* to Kate and ask if she was having a good time in Toronto.

Lucern felt himself tensing as he waited for her answer. He was vaguely surprised when she laughed and said, "Oh, yes."

Etienne seemed equally surprised. He asked, "You mean, my brother is actually entertaining you?" As if Lucern were some sort of heathen, incapable of being a good host.

"Yes." Kate nodded cheerfully. "He and your mother, too. Marguerite took me shopping and to the spa today. And last night, Lucern and I played Blood Lust Two until all hours of the morning."

"Oh!" Rachel exclaimed. "Isn't that a wonderful game? Etienne is so talented. Although I thought he'd drive me crazy with it when he was designing the end sequence. It gave him trouble."

"Etienne?" Kate glanced from Rachel to Etienne uncertainly.

"Yes. It's his game," Rachel explained. Then she glanced at her brother-in-law with surprise. "Didn't you tell her it was Etienne's game?"

"Yes, I'm sure I mentioned—"

"No, you didn't!" Kate exclaimed with a light slap at his arm. "Oh, my God! Why didn't you tell me?"

Lucern scowled. His editor didn't notice; she'd already turned back to his brother.

"I can't believe it! I love Blood Lust, both One and Two. They are amazing!"

She rambled on, gushing over Etienne in a way Lucern found annoying, then suddenly stopped with a small gasp, before saying, "Oh! I just realized, the primary characters in Luc's last book were named Rachel and Etienne. And Etienne was a game creator, too. Oh, wow." She gave a laugh and grinned at Rachel. "The next thing you'll tell me is that you're a coroner like the woman in the book."

Lucern, Etienne and Rachel all exchanged glances and shifted uncomfortably.

Kate's eyes widened at their silence. "You aren't, are you?"

"I like to base stories as much in reality as I can," Lucern said to break the silence.

"But you write vampire books." Kate sounded bewildered.

"Well, within reason," he amended, then took her arm firmly. "Come. We're holding up the line."

Lucern hurried Kate to his car, saw her inside, got in himself and immediately turned the radio on. He cranked the volume up high to prevent conversation and drove to the reception hall where the wedding dinner was to be held. In his rush to get there, where he hoped Kate would be distracted and forget the odd co-incidence of the characters in his books matching his real-life family, Lucern somewhat exceeded the speed limit. As a result, they were one of the first to arrive.

Much to his relief, Kate didn't mention the matter again. She and Lucern were seated at a table, and his mother and his sister Lissianna with her husband Greg soon joined them. Bastien was seated at the head table with the rest of the wedding party, so it was just the five of them at the six-person table closest to the long head table.

Lucern spent the first several minutes simply finger-ing the glass of wine that was promptly set before him, his gaze darting nervously to Kate as she talked with Marguerite and Lissianna. The three women were mak-ing him terribly nervous. They had their heads together, and there seemed to be an awful lot of giggling and laughing mixed in with their quiet talking. He was dying to know what they were saying, but couldn't have heard had he tried, with all the talk and disruption as people arrived and greeted one another.

"Lissianna!"

Lucern stiffened at his editor's exclamation; then Kate turned on him. "Your sister's name is Lissianna! That's the name of the female vampire in your second book."

"Er . . . yes." He shot a glance at his mother and sister. Were they deliberately trying to complicate his life?

"Etienne and Rachel in the last book, Lissianna and Greg in the second. And Marguerite!" She turned on

Lucern's mother. "Your husband was named Claude, wasn't he?"

"It's pronounced with an 'o' sound dear, like load, not 'ah' like clod," Marguerite corrected gently. Then she nodded. "But, yes, my husband and my children's father was Claude."

"Oh." Kate was silent for a moment, but was obviously thinking, looking for other similarities. "And your family name is Argeneau, too. No, wait," she corrected herself. "In the novels it's Argentus, from the Latin 'argent' for silver, because the patriarch had silvery blue eyes. Like you!" She turned suddenly to peer into Lucern's eyes.

"Yes." Lucern shifted, feeling terribly uncomfortable, unsure how to explain. In the end, he didn't need to.

"I think it's terribly sweet of you to name your characters after your family like that," Kate said.

Lucern gaped at her in surprise. Sweet? He wasn't sweet. What the—

"It's obvious you care for them a great deal."

"Er . . ." Lucern was feeling oddly trapped when a tap on his shoulder drew his head around. He found himself staring at Bastien and Etienne. Relief at the distraction made him smile hugely, which surprised them.

"We need a hand from both of you." Bastien's look encompassed both Lucern and Greg.

"Oh. Oh, of course." Luc turned to Kate as Greg got to his feet. "They need us. We have to go," he explained.

Kate nodded solemnly. "It's a guy thing, huh?"

"Er . . . yes." Luc stood, tossed a warning glare at his mother and sister, lest they say something else to put

weird ideas in Kate's head, then followed his brothers
away from the table.

The foursome crossed the reception hall, left through
a door half-hidden behind a decorated beam, walked
up a long, narrow hall, then exited through another
door that led into the parking lot behind the building.
Bastien walked along the row of parked vehicles to his
van. Lucern didn't know what was going on until his
brother opened the back doors and dragged a medi-
vac cooler closer.

"I don't know about you guys, but with everything
that had to be done, I didn't get to feed before the
wedding today. I thought I might not be the only one
with that problem, so I packed a picnic for us." Bastien
popped the cooler open.

Lucern grinned at the sight of the blood bags packed
in ice. Good old Bastien. He was always prepared. He
would have been a Boy Scout as a child had they had
them in those days.

"Oh, thank God!" Etienne took the first bag Bastien
held out. "I was so busy rushing around, I didn't get a
chance to feed. Neither did Rachel, I'm sure."

"I brought enough for everyone," Bastien assured
him. He handed bags to both Lucern and Greg. "I'll
bring the ladies out after we go back. I just didn't think
it would be good if we all left en masse. The Argeneau
side would understand, but the Garretts would be confused."

"Too true, my friend," Greg said with a shake of his
head. "I'm still not used to all this." He gestured to the
bag in his hand, then lifted it and stabbed his elongat-
ing teeth into it.

87

Lucern smiled as he followed suit. For someone who claimed the opposite, his brother-in-law did a fair imitation of someone who was comfortable with his new situation. Mind you, that might be different if the therapist had to bite people to feed, as in the old days.

The four men all fell silent as they emptied their first bags of blood. Bastien then pulled plastic cups out of the van and split two more bags between those four cups, and the men stood talking as they drank. It wasn't long before the conversation came around to Lucern's unwanted guest. Etienne was the one to bring it up, commenting that she seemed quite nice.

Lucern snorted. "Don't let her fool you. That woman is as stubborn as a mule. She's like one of those damn ticks, burrowing under your skin and staying there. She's burrowed her way into my home and just won't leave!"

The others all laughed. Greg suggested, "Why don't you just do some of that mind-control stuff Lissianna's trying to teach me—just get into her head and plant the suggestion that she leave?"

"Luc can't get into her head," Etienne announced with a grin.

"You've tried?" Greg asked Lucern with surprise.

"Of course I did. The very first night." Luc scowled and shook his head. "But she seems resistant to suggestion. I can't even read her thoughts. The woman's mind is like a steel trap." He sighed. "It's damned frustrating."

"Yep. And don't tell Mother," Etienne reminded him.

"Why not?" Greg asked.

Bastien explained. "Mother says couples shouldn't be

able to read each other's thoughts, so when you come across someone strong-minded enough to block you out—which she says is rare—you should pay attention, they would make a good mate."

Etienne nodded. "So if she catches wind of this . . ."

"She'll be determined to put us together," Lucern finished for him. He immediately felt confused. The last thing he needed was his mother playing matchmaker and forcing him and his stubborn editor together. On the other hand, Kate was a hell of a game player. And she was attractive, and somehow she became less annoying the longer he knew her. He was even getting used to having her in his home. If he were going to be forced into marriage—

"So I wouldn't mention it to her if I were you," Bastien said.

"I'd have to agree with Bastien and Etienne on this," Gregory decided, looking at Lucern. "As much as I like your mother, she can be a tad persistent once she gets an idea into her head. If you don't want her interfering and trying to push you and Kate together, I wouldn't mention that you can't read Kate's mind."

"Too late."

All four men jumped guiltily at that sweetly sung comment. Whirling, they found themselves confronted by Marguerite. Lucern groaned at the predatory look on her face. She'd obviously heard everything. And judging by her expression, she was already plotting.

At least that was what he thought, so he was surprised when she took the bag of blood Bastien offered and turned to smile at her oldest son. "Luc, darling. If you want to get rid of the girl so badly, why not just agree to do one of the publicity things she's on about? The moment you agree, she'll leave."

" 'Cause I don't want to," he answered, almost wincing as he heard how childish he sounded.

"And I don't want to listen to you whine, but sometimes we have to do things we don't like in life." Her words made everyone fall silent; then Marguerite stabbed her teeth into her bag of blood and drained it. When she'd finished, she turned to Lucern and added, "Kate doesn't want to be here bothering you any more than you want her here. However, her job depends on being able to convince you to do one of those publicity events. She likes her new position. She wants to keep it. She won't leave until you agree to at least one."

Spotting his horrified reaction, Marguerite patted her son's cheek affectionately. "I suggest you tell her you'll do R.T. From what she told me at the spa today, it's probably the best option for both of you."

"What's R.T.?" Lucern asked suspiciously.

"*Romantic Times* magazine," his mother explained. "Just tell her you'll do it." Then Marguerite Argeneau turned and walked away, heading back along the row of cars.

"Hmm. I wonder how she found out Kate's job depends on convincing you to do one of those publicity events," Bastien murmured as they watched their mother walk away.

Greg shrugged. "She's very good at getting people to tell her things they never mean to say. She would have made a good therapist."

Lucern was silent, and they all handed their empty glasses back to Bastien. He didn't know how his mother had found out what she had, but he didn't doubt for a minute that it was true. Which made him about as miserable as he could be, for now he knew for certain that he would never be free of the woman. She was desperate, and desperate people were both as persistent as hell and unpredictable.

"Here you all are!"

The four men whirled away from the van again, this time to find Kate C. Leever facing them. There was a mischievous grin on her face as she took in their guilty expressions and the way they were all trying to hide something behind them.

"Rachel was looking for you. I said I thought I saw you come out here and said I'd check for her," she explained, still eyeing them with amusement. "She tried to stop me and said she'd go, but it's her wedding—I couldn't let her leave her guests to go chasing after you four reprobates."

Lucern exchanged a glance with the others. They all knew darned well that Rachel had probably hoped to slip outside for a quick nip as their mother had just done. Kate, in her kindness, had made that impossible.

"Why did you call us reprobates?" Gregory asked.

Kate gave an airy wave and laughed. "Because of what you're doing out here."

The four men exchanged glances and shifted into a tighter group, making sure that the open back of the van and the cooler of blood were hidden; then Lucern echoed, "What we're doing?"

"Oh, like it isn't obvious," she snorted. "Sneaking out here, crowding around the van." She shook her head and gave them a condescending look. "I may have been raised in Nebraska, but I've lived in New York long enough to be savvy about you artist types."

Now the looks the men exchanged were bewildered. Artist types? Lucern was a writer, Etienne a program developer, Bastien a businessman and Greg was a therapist. Artist types? And what did she think artist types did anyway? The only way to find out was to ask. Lucern did. "What is it exactly that you think we are doing out here?"

She gave a resigned sigh. "You're smoking pot-joints." She said it as one word.

The men all gaped at her; then Etienne released a disbelieving laugh. "What?"

Kate tsked with exasperation. "Pot. Marijuana. You guys snuck out here for a debbie."

"Er . . . I believe it's called a doobie," Greg interjected.

"Whatever. That's what you were doing, right?"

"Er . . ." Lucern began. Then he, Bastien, Etienne and Greg shared a grin.

"Yes. You caught us. We were smoking a debbie," Etienne agreed.

"Doobie," Greg corrected.

"Yes." Bastien nodded. "We'd offer you some, but we . . . er . . ."

"Smoked it all up," Etienne finished.

The two men sounded disgustingly apologetic to Lucern's mind. Good Lord.

"Oh, that's okay. I don't smoke anything." She smiled crookedly, then added, "Besides, dinner is about to be served. I think that's why Rachel was looking for you."

"Well then, we should go in." Stepping forward, Lucern took Kate's arm firmly and turned her toward the building. They'd barely taken two steps when he heard the van doors closing and the other men fell into step behind them. *Smoking debbies. Good Lord.*

Lucern was distracted through dinner, merely picking at the food. It was apparently very good, if Kate's comments were to be believed, but he didn't really have an appetite. He found his mind stuck on his mother's claim that Kate's job depended on her convincing him to cooperate. Lucern didn't know why, but that was really bothering him. A lot.

". . . dance, Luc."

Lucern glanced around in confusion. He'd only caught the end of his mother's words, he'd been so deep in thought. He peered at her in question. "What?"

"I said, you should take Kate out on the floor and dance. To support Etienne and Rachel. Someone has to start everyone else dancing."

He glanced toward the dance floor, surprised to see that the bride and groom were dancing. The meal was over, and the first dance had begun. He, as the head of his side of the family, would be expected to join next. By all rights, he should be taking his mother, the matriarch, up there to encourage others to dance, but one look at Marguerite told him that she had started her matchmaking in earnest. She would not be dancing with him.

Sighing, he pushed his seat back and held out a hand to Kate. His editor looked terribly uncertain as she placed her fingers in his and rose—a fact that annoyed him no end, for reasons he couldn't possibly fathom and had no intention of examining too deeply. Telling himself it was just a duty dance, and that his mother couldn't force him to dance with Kate again, Lucern led her onto the dance floor and took her into his arms.

It was a mistake. Kate C. Leever fit in his arms as if she'd been made for him. Her head came up just short of Lucern's chin, her hand was small and soft in his, and the scent of her perfume wafted tantalizing and vaguely exciting to his nose. Without even realizing it, he found himself urging her closer so that his body could meld with hers, his legs and chest brushing her with every step.

Lucern was used to hunger; he experienced it every morning upon awakening. While he slept, his body processed the blood he drank, repairing whatever damage the day had wrought and leaving him dehydrated and in serious need of more. Some days that hunger was worse than others. Some days it was mild enough that he could be distracted by other things as he had been this morning. Still, Lucern knew hunger. He understood thirst. He lived daily with a bone-deep yearning that could become so strong his body would cramp with it. And yet this . . .

He lowered his head, breathing in the scent of Kate's shampoo mingled with the spice and sweetness of her perfume. She smelled vaguely of vanilla, like a rich and luscious dessert or a bowl of ice cream, and he had the sudden mad urge to lick the nape of her neck and . . .

Lucern straightened abruptly as he caught hold of his thoughts. Lick her nape? More like bite it. Good Lord, he needed more blood. He'd been rather slack on the consumption end lately. What with Kate's presence and such, he hadn't been sticking to his usual four pints a day. He'd been running on mostly two—which explained his odd hunger now. He was confusing hunger for Kate's blood with hunger for her.

Relieved beyond measure, he smiled widely down at her when she murmured his name. She seemed slightly surprised at his smile, then asked uncertainly, "Is something wrong? You've stopped dancing."

Lucern peered around, surprised to realize that in his revelation he had stopped moving. He now merely stood in the middle of the dance floor holding her close. Very close. Her breasts, squashed against his chest, were being forced upward out of her gown. And they were very nice breasts. Round and a pale pink flesh tone that spoke of healthy blood. Lucern would have liked to lick his way over those orbs and . . .

"I have to talk to Bastien," he gasped. "Now."

Releasing her from his tight hold, he started to walk to where Bastien was dancing, then suddenly realized what he was doing. Whirling back to the bewildered Kate, who stood like an abandoned baby in the center of the dance floor, he took her arm and led her back to their table. He then walked around the dance floor, relieved that the music ended just as he reached his brother's side.

"Bastien, after you've seen your dance partner back to the table, I need to talk to you outside. At the van," he said meaningfully.

"Sure," his younger brother said. "Be with you in a moment."

Lucern nodded, and Bastien walked Rachel's sister, who was the maid of honor, back to the head table.

"Did I hear you say you were going out to the van?"

Lucern turned to find Lissianna behind him. She and Gregory had joined the dance floor just after Lucern and Kate. The couple had been standing nearby, waiting for the next song to start. He wasn't surprised she'd heard what he said.

He nodded in answer to her question, and felt it necessary to explain: "I haven't been feeding enough since Kate arrived."

Lissianna nodded in understanding. "Rachel and I will join the two of you. She was saying earlier that, what with preparing for the wedding and everything, she—"

"Fine, fine," Lucern interrupted. He didn't need the explanation. He was happy to have the women join them. "Go get her, then. Bastien will . . . Oh. He's brought her with him."

Bastien was leading their new sister-in-law across the floor.

"I'll keep an eye on Kate, so she doesn't come out and try to catch you with the debbies in hand," Greg said lightly as Bastien and the bride arrived. He moved off to invite the editor to dance.

"Good, good." Lucern didn't even smile. He just nodded his thanks and ushered the other three out of the reception hall.

Kate relaxed in Greg's arms the moment they started to move, something she hadn't been able to do in Lucern's embrace. She had seen the writer slip outside with his sister, Rachel and Bastien, and suspected they were out there smoking again. In her considered opinion, the man could use it. It would help him relax, surely. The man had been tense throughout the meal, and . . . Well, she supposed he had just seemed distracted through the meal—not that she'd let it bother her. She'd been busy talking to his mother and sister and listening to the amusing tales they told her about Lucern's youth.

If the mother and sister were to be believed, Lucern was really a very sensitive man with a crusty, grumpy shell. Having read his novels, Kate thought that was quite possible. There was a certain longing in the way he portrayed the couples in his book, a hunger that went beyond the bloodlust of vampires or even beyond sexual desire. His characters were lonely at heart, yearning for a soul mate to share their long lives. Kate wondered now if it wasn't a reflection of his feelings, if he didn't yearn for love.

Greg gave her a little twirl, and she smiled at him. Lissianna's husband was a much more relaxed dancer than Lucern. Luc had been almost vibrating with tension as he and she had moved across the dance floor, and it had transferred to Kate, filling her with a low-grade tension that was rather distressing. Despite that tension, however, she'd found herself melting into his embrace, resting her head on his shoulder and slipping her fingers closer to the nape of his neck to brush the hair there. She'd been relieved if a little stunned when he'd stopped dancing and walked away.

Well, all right, she'd been more stunned than relieved. She had stood there, gaping after him, unable to believe that he was reverting to his trademark rudeness right there in the middle of the dance floor for all to see. If he hadn't suddenly turned back and seen her to their table, she might have chased him down and given him a swift kick to the behind. Yes, it was definitely a good thing he was outside smoking. Surely it would relax him.

"I think you should just agree to do something for her," Bastien suggested. Of course, as ever, Kate had been the topic of conversation since they'd reached the van. And much to Lucern's irritation, everyone seemed to have advice.

"Why don't you tell her you'll do one of those interviews? Like that R.T. thing Mom suggested," Bastien continued. "Or tell her you'll do one of the publicity events, but only one and not the book-signing tour. Let her choose which is most likely to save her job. That way, she'll be happy and leave."

"Let *her* choose?" Lucern was horrified at the idea of giving her so much sway. "But what if she chooses one of the television interviews?"

Lissianna clucked impatiently. "It wouldn't kill you to spend half an hour in front of a camera, Luc."

"But—"

"Look at it this way," his sister added. "Half an hour in front of a camera during an interview, or Kate Leever camping out on your porch."

Bastien laughed. "If you even manage to get her out the front door."

Lucern glared at him, but his brother merely shrugged. "You've apparently gone soft on us, Luc," he continued. "A hundred years ago you wouldn't have had any trouble tossing her out on her heart-shaped little behind."

"You've been looking at her behind?" Lucern asked in outrage.

"Sure, why not? She's single. I'm single." He shrugged. "Is there a problem?"

Lucern scowled. There shouldn't be a problem, and he knew it. But for some reason, he didn't like Bastien checking out Kate at all.

"Poor Luc," Lissianna said. He peered at her in question, so she patted his arm as if he needed soothing. "Six hundred years old, and you just don't know how to deal with the feelings Kate raises in you. Surely with age some wisdom should come."

"It seems men remain emotionally dense no matter how long they live," Rachel commented dryly.

Lucern remained silent, his thoughts in an uproar. Lissianna was implying he was unaware he was falling for the girl. He wasn't. He was aware of it. But he didn't have to like it—or give in to it, either. As to the hunger he felt around her, Lucern admitted now it wasn't bloodlust he'd felt on the dance floor, but sexual lust. He wanted Kate C. Leever, editor. And that was a complication he could do without. If her mind wasn't closed to him, he might have been willing to indulge himself and enjoy her body as he wanted to. He certainly hadn't lived as a monk for six hundred years. But her mind *was* closed, making such an action dangerous.

Shaking his head, he left the others by the van and headed back into the reception hall. As far as he was concerned, he was just suffering a crush—a natural affection caused by being forced into close proximity with someone else. He'd get over it just as soon as Kate C. Leever was gone. He just had to get her gone.

Chapter Six

Marguerite was the only one at the table when Lucern returned and reclaimed his seat. A quick scan of the dance floor showed Kate and Greg were dancing. They looked awfully cozy. Kate was relaxed and smiling in Gregory Hewitt's arms—something she hadn't been in Lucern's—and they were moving in perfect sync, as if they'd been dancing together for years.

Gregory even looked pretty damned suave out there on the dance floor. Lucern had never thought of his brother-in-law as a ladies' man, but he certainly seemed to be doing a pretty good imitation right now. Logically, Lucern knew Greg loved Lissianna deeply and was no threat when it came to Kate. Besides which, Lucern reminded himself quickly, he himself wasn't even interested in a relationship with the woman. But his body didn't appear to be responding to his logic. Some primal part of him didn't give a hoot for logic. And as he watched Greg whirl Kate around the dance floor, Lucern could feel his muscles tensing and twitching. A low growl rumbled to life in his chest as he watched the pair dip and then recover.

"You should go cut in."

Lucern stiffened at his mother's words. He glanced her way and saw she was casting a pitying look upon him. He turned sharply, struggled briefly with himself, then jerked to his feet and strode onto the dance floor. If there was anything Lucern hated it was being pitied. Now he was mad.

Greg noticed his approach, took one look at his expression, nodded solemnly and quit the dance floor.

Kate turned in confusion when Greg suddenly released her and stepped away. She supposed she wasn't surprised to see Lucern there. However, she was surprised at his expression. His usually cold, grumpy exterior had been replaced by the intensity of a stalking animal. He looked hard and angry, but not cold. Anything but cold. His eyes were all silver with no blue. She now understood a description he had given of Claude in his first book: "Flinty eyes that spoke of the fires of hell and left his enemies quailing." She hadn't imagined that silver-blue eyes could look so ferocious, but there were vermilion fires burning there, almost seeming to snap out of his irises like the arc from a welder's flame.

Yet Kate wasn't afraid. For some reason a smile curved her lips, and she couldn't have stopped the words that popped out had she tried. "Smoking debbies didn't relax you, I take it?"

Lucern reacted as if he crashed into an invisible wall. His determined stride broke at once, and he stared at her with a blank expression that utterly erased the feral fever of moments before. Then he did the most amazing thing: Lucern Argeneau, that stubborn, stupid, ignorant man, actually let loose a gale of laughter. In truth, Kate hadn't thought such a thing possible. The man was such a . . .

Her thoughts died as he swept her into his arms and they began to dance. He was still chuckling softly, the action making his chest reverberate against hers. He urged her closer. When Kate lifted her head to peer shyly into his face, he smiled and said, "You're an evil woman, Kate C. Leever."

She found herself smiling in return. She had thought the man handsome from the first, but now, with laughter sparkling in his eyes and tilting the corners of his mouth, he was so much more than simply handsome. He was breathtaking. Literally. Kate honestly had some difficulty breathing as she met his gaze. Heat was radiating from every point their bodies met. She wanted to lay her head on his shoulder and melt into him. She wanted to feel his hands move over her flesh. She wanted . . .

To go home. Kate definitely wanted to go home. Or, really, she wanted to go anywhere that would take her far away from him. She didn't want to feel this way, she didn't want to want him. Hell, she didn't even like the man.

Well, all right, she admitted with painful honesty; she'd had fun playing Blood Lust Two with him, and he *could* be nice when he tried. She was sure. It wasn't as if he had tried yet. But surely everyone could be nice with a little effort? Yes, she assured herself. In fact, he was being nice to her right now. Sort of.

Kate sighed to herself. Dancing certainly felt nice. And when Lucern held her like this, she forgot how rude and pigheaded he could be. But—and it was a big but—she had absolutely no intention of getting involved with one of her writers. She was a businesswoman. A professional. And she would act professionally even if that's all it was, an act, and she really wanted to rip his designer suit off and plaster herself to his naked body.

Ohhhh. This wasn't good.

Lucern suddenly stopped dancing and announced, "I'm tired." When she didn't respond, he added, "Are you ready to leave?"

"Yes." She fired off the response like a bullet. She was more than happy to escape the possibility of suffering any more of this closeness.

Lucern apparently agreed. He immediately took her arm, led her off the floor and across the hall. He stopped only once, pausing briefly at the head table to tell his brother and new sister-in-law that they were leaving.

Kate spied Marguerite Argeneau frowning at them from her seat at the table they had shared, and she knew Lucern's mother wasn't pleased that they were leaving so early. She felt bad, but really it wasn't her problem. Marguerite was Lucern's problem. Kate's problem was maintaining a businesslike relationship while getting Lucern to do a publicity event. And she only had one more day to do it.

* * *

104

Lucern was silent on the way home, his thoughts a bit muddled. He wasn't certain what his intentions had been when he'd suggested leaving early, but . . .

Oh, who was he kidding? He'd been thinking about getting Kate home alone and possibly naked. The woman had gotten under his skin, and his family had made him admit it. Bastien had given him a nudge with the comment about her behind, and with the knowing smile on his face when he'd asked if his noticing was a problem; then Lissianna had made it worse with her "poor Luc." Just the sight of Kate in Greg's arms had roused the beast inside. But the look of pity on his mother's face had been the worst. Lucern realized that he could try to fool himself, but he was fooling no one else. And hell, he wasn't even fooling himself.

He liked her. Despite the fact that she was a modern woman, pushy and aggressive when necessary, who simply did not know her place, he liked her. Despite the fact that she seemed to have no dragons to slay, except perhaps him and his lack of cooperation, he liked her. And, dear God, he *wanted* her.

Lucern was a healthy male of 612 years. The number of women he'd been with in that time . . . Well, he couldn't even guess at the number. However, every single one had faded from his mind when he held Kate in his arms.

But she wasn't in his arms now; she was seated in the passenger seat, arms crossed defensively over her chest and staring blindly into the night as they drove. She was deliberately ignoring him, distancing herself. It helped to clear Luc's mind somewhat. Kate was his editor. He had to work with her. Sleeping with her would be a giant no-no. He felt inexpressibly weary as he pulled into his driveway.

Both he and Kate were silent as they got out of the car. She was the first to speak. She gazed up at the star-studded sky as they walked up the drive and murmured, "It's a beautiful night."

Lucern's steps faltered at her wistful tone. She sounded reluctant to see the night end, and he didn't want it to, either. Lucern knew he couldn't give in to his desire for her, but he was still loath to part from her.

"It *is* nice," he agreed. "Would you like to sit on the porch and have a glass of wine?"

He held his breath as she hesitated.

"Can we have coffee instead?" she asked. "I've had more than my usual quota of alcohol tonight."

Lucern let his breath out in a whoosh. "Certainly. Sit down and I'll—"

"I'll help." She smiled for the first time since they'd left the reception. "No offense, but I don't think you've made a lot of coffee."

Lucern wasn't offended. He was just happy that the evening wasn't going to end and that Kate C. Leever was smiling.

They worked in a companionable silence in the kitchen, Kate making coffee while he found bowls and scooped out some ice cream. Then they took their treasure out to the porch.

Kate stared up at the stars in the sky. It was such a peaceful night, so beautiful, and she was actually enjoying Lucern's company. Yes, she was actually enjoying it. His usual grumpy, terse persona was missing. She didn't know if it was the alcohol or the debbies he had smoked at the wedding that had done it, but for the first time, he seemed very mellow in her presence. Oh, he had been pleasant the night before when they'd played the game together, but this was different. He'd been tense and ready to shoot the video-game bad guys then. Now he was incredibly relaxed and a pleasure to be with. They sat there for quite a while, drinking, eating their ice cream and chatting mildly about the wedding while avoiding looking at each other. At least Kate was avoiding looking at him. She had to—every time she gazed on the smile flirting on his lips, she wanted to kiss it.

You're a fool, Kate told herself. Her attraction to Lucern Argeneau was dangerous, and she shouldn't be encouraging it by suffering him being nice and even likeable. He was *one of her writers*. She was like a den mother to her authors. But her feelings for Lucern at the moment were far from maternal. And the longer this nice interlude went on, the harder it got for her to resist moving closer, touching him as she talked, leaning into him, kissing . . .

Cutting off her thoughts right there, she straightened and sought something to distract herself, something to end this interlude. The easiest solution was the reason for her being there. Kate took a deep breath, then blurted, "Luc, I know you don't want to talk about this, but I really wish you would consider a book-signing tour."

The writer tensed at once, the softness in his features disappearing. "No. I quite simply don't do book-signing tours."

107

"I know you don't, Luc. But . . . your books are so popular and—"

"Then I hardly need to do a tour, do I?"

"But the readers want to meet you, they—"

"No," he repeated firmly.

"Luc, please," Kate entreated, her voice husky.

Lucern stared at Kate silently, wishing with all his heart that what she was pleading for was something entirely different. *Luc, please kiss me. Luc, please take me to your bed. Luc, please* . . . But that wasn't what she was asking for. This was business. A desire for him to promote his books and make more money for her company. She wanted him to disrupt his life, risk the day with its damaging sunlight, and do a book-signing tour. Lucern wished he'd never written those damn popular books.

Standing, he abruptly tossed the rest of his coffee on the lawn and headed for the door. "I have work to do. Good night."

"No, wait. Lucern!" She was on her feet and after him at once. "We have to discuss this. I've been here three days and I haven't gotten a thing done."

Lucern ignored her. He merely stepped inside and started upstairs.

"Luc, please! None of the writers like book-signings, but they are so good for publicity, and readers want the contact. They want to meet the writer behind the stories they enjoy so much. Just a short tour would do," she wheedled when he made no response. "Half a dozen stops, maybe. I could go with you to be sure everything was just the way you wanted. If you would only—"

Lucern reached his office door. He stepped inside

and closed it behind him with a bang that was only slightly louder than the click of the lock.

Kate stared at the door. Slammed doors seemed to be a recurring theme in their relationship. She was beginning to hate doors.

Shoulders slumping, she leaned against the door and closed her eyes. She was a very positive person as a rule, and had always thought that a person could do anything they set their mind to if they worked at it hard enough, but that was before she'd met the immovable object: Lucern. The man was as stubborn as . . . well, as she was. Maybe more.

Kate considered giving up, packing her bags and heading back to New York with her tail between her legs, but it wasn't in her nature. She hated to be such a pest and wished she could just leave him to his peaceful existence, but in the company's opinion it wasn't unreasonable for them to expect Lucern Argeneau to do some promotion. They put out big bucks to advertise his books; the least he could do was put in a little effort himself. And she mostly agreed with that. She just had to convince him. Hell, at this point she'd consider it a grand victory just to get him to agree to a couple of interviews over the phone.

Kate straightened slowly. It might work. She'd been concentrating on the book-signing tour, but perhaps she would have more luck with interviews.

"Luc?" she called out. Silence was her answer, but Kate wasn't deterred. "Look, I know you don't want to do the book-signing tour, and that's fine. But, please, at least consider doing a couple of interviews?"

She waited in the silence, then added, "Just think about it. Okay?"

Deciding to leave it for the night, Kate turned to the guest room door. She had to think of an argument, some plan to persuade him. Then she'd tackle him again in the morning.

Lucern knew when Kate gave up and walked away. He felt her absence as well as heard the opening and closing of the guest room door. He sat for a long time at his desk listening to her moving around getting ready for bed, then to the sounds of the night when she stopped.

He considered playing Blood Lust II, but it wasn't the same without her. He considered writing but wasn't in the mood. So he sat there in the silent darkness, listening to the night. The cry of night birds, the song of crickets, the whisper of the wind, the sighs of. . . . Kate, he realized. That sleepy breathy sound had been Kate. Lucern could just hear it if he strained. He could smell her, too. The scent seemed to hang about him. Recalling her leaning against him as they danced, he ducked his head and sniffed his jacket. The scent was strong there. Disturbing.

Standing, Lucern shrugged off the jacket and slung it over the back of his chair, but the smell still seemed to cling to him. Or perhaps it was simply in the air, perhaps permeating his home just as she had. Giving up on trying to rid himself of her scent, he moved to unlock the door of his office and open it; then he stood there and closed his eyes. If he concentrated hard, the other night sounds faded and he was able to focus on the sound of her—the rustle of bedclothes as she shifted, soft little sighs as she dreamt, an occasional murmur, but mostly her breathing, soft and soothing, in, out, over and over again.

He could almost feel her breath against his skin, a warm, moist exhalation. Then he realized he *was* feeling it, soft and warm against his hand. He was standing next to the bed, his legs having carried him where his body longed to be—and all without his brain's awareness.

Lucern stared down at her through the moonlit gloom, smiling at the childlike way she slept. Kate was curled into a fetal position on her side, her hand tucked under her chin. Then his gaze drifted away from her face and down over her body. It was a warm night, and the air-conditioning didn't seem to reach the upstairs rooms as well as the lower ones. Kate had kicked off the sheets and lay in a thin white cotton nightie that had twisted up around her thighs. His gaze skimmed her slender limbs in their bent position. Kate had lovely legs, long and shapely. Luc managed to resist the temptation to run his fingers lightly over the pearly white skin revealed, but imagined what it must be like and knew it would be warm and soft to the touch.

A feathery sigh slipped from Kate's lips and she rolled onto her back in her sleep, one hand sliding slowly across her breasts before dropping to lie on the bed. Lucern followed the movement of the hand, then returned his eyes along the trail her hand had taken to settle at the neckline of her gown. The gown had buttons leading down to her waist. The top two were undone, and the third appeared ready to slip its hole, leaving a large expanse bare to view. Luc's gaze fastened on the milky tops of her breasts, and he watched them rise and fall with each breath. Rise and fall. He imagined freeing that third button to reveal more skin, then another and another, at last baring her breasts fully.

Lucern imagined how round and full they would appear in the moonlight. How luscious. He knew he wouldn't be able to resist touching them, caressing them, taking one hardening nipple into his mouth and suckling at its sweetness.

Kate arched in the bed and moaned low in her throat. Lucern almost moaned with her. Her perfume was stronger in here; it mixed with the smells of her shampoo and soap and essence. The combination was heady. He could taste it on his lips. Except for the lack of touch, he could imagine he really was: suckling, licking, nibbling a path across her skin from one breast to the other.

Lucern closed his eyes to imagine it better and could almost feel her warm skin beneath his lips. In his mind, he let his hands skim down her gown, slip beneath, then feather up the outsides of her thighs. He could feel her shudder under his touch, shift her legs restlessly as another moan sighed from her lips. Kate arched in invitation, wanting him, too—begging him to fill her and make her whole, to quench the fire he'd started.

Lucern was happy to oblige. He allowed his imaginary hands to drift over the tops of her legs, to push the flimsy cloth of her gown upward, then spread her soft thighs so that he could lick the vein there. He imagined touching her, caressing her, licking her glistening skin, then driving himself into her hot, welcoming body. He

112

could almost feel her close around him, gasping and whimpering in his ear, her breath soft on his skin, her nails scoring his shoulders and back.

Kate would moan with pleasure as he drove into her over and over until she began to shake and shudder beneath him, her inner muscles clenching and unclenching.

"Lucern."

His name on her lips drew his eyes open, and he peered down to find Kate's sleeping face a portrait of ecstasy. She was panting, sweating and writhing on the sheets, her hands on either side of her head and tearing at the pillow as she convulsed with ecstasy. It was only then Lucern realized that while her mind was closed to him when she was awake, it was as wide open as anyone else's in rest. She'd just experienced everything he'd imagined, received it from his mind as if it were happening.

The knowledge was almost painful. He could have her if he wished. She would welcome him. Luc was breathing heavily with want, throbbing with desire, aching to drive himself into her. At the same moment, he yearned to fasten his teeth to her neck, consume her blood and body both at once. He knew it would be the most incredible experience of his life. But he couldn't. If he took her now, Kate would welcome it only because he wanted her to want him.

Shaking his head to erase the erotic images there, Lucern stumbled back from the bed, then out of her room. He didn't stop, but staggered drunkenly down the hall to the stairs. His head was full of her. He had to get away. The desire to take her was overwhelming.

He slammed out of the house and to his car. He had no plans when he started the engine, simply needed to get away from Kate and the temptation she presented. He ended up driving around for an hour or so before finally finding himself in Bastien's driveway. His brother's house was dark and silent, and he could sense that it was empty. He was about to back out of the driveway when Bastien's van pulled in beside him.

Lucern got out with relief, met his brother at the front of the vehicles and blurted out his troubles with Kate. It took a long while. He told his younger brother everything.

When he had finished, Bastien merely asked, "What will you do?"

Lucern was silent for a moment. Talking hadn't helped him clear his mind. He was still confused. He disliked confusion. He disliked any sort of disruption in his life. The answer seemed simple: Get rid of the confusion.

"I'm going to do whatever it takes to get her on a plane tomorrow," he decided.

There. Talking to his brother *had* helped.

Kate yawned and stretched in bed, a smile playing about her lips. She hadn't slept so well in ages. And she hadn't ever woken up feeling so great. She was so relaxed, so sated. Blinking in surprise, she realized it was true—she felt sated. Her body was a happy body, all warm and ready to do whatever she wanted.

Getting up, she got into the shower. It wasn't until she was humming and washing herself, running soap over her body, that she recalled the dream. Her hands slowed, her eyes dilating as the memories crowded in: Lucern caressing her, suckling her breasts, thrusting his body into hers.

A tingling drew her gaze down to her breasts, and she let her hands drop with embarrassment as she realized she'd unconsciously been caressing them. Her nipples were hard and erect. Even worse, she could feel the wetness building between her legs, and it had nothing to do with the shower at her back. Turning into the spray, she braced her hands on the shower wall beneath the nozzle head and allowed the water to pour across her body. But the dream didn't fade away—it was the most vivid she could ever recall having.

For one minute, Kate was afraid that it hadn't been a dream, that it had really happened and just seemed like a dream because she had been sleepy. But then she shook her head at the silly thought. If it had really happened, she would have wanted kisses, and he hadn't kissed her once. Kate would have grabbed him by a handful of hair and dragged his mouth to hers if necessary, but she would have had kisses. She liked kisses.

No, it hadn't happened, she thought, giggling as relief poured through her. It had just been an amazingly sexy dream. A *wet* dream.

Laughing at herself, Kate finished her shower and stepped out to dry herself. Dream or not, she felt great. She was also feeling rather benevolent toward her host for the pleasure of the dream. It didn't matter that he'd had nothing to do with it; he'd been the star of the dream, and in that dream he had given her great pleasure. Yep. He was a swell guy.

115

Smiling widely, Kate dressed, brushed her hair, then left her room and jogged downstairs to the kitchen. She was going to make Lucern some breakfast. A big breakfast. And she was going to sweetly tell him she'd given up on trying to get him to do the book-signing tour. Maybe then he'd be so relieved, he'd agree to do an interview or two.

She made the works: steak so rare it was still bleeding, eggs over easy, hash browns, toast and coffee. Then she was in a quandary. What to do? There was no sign of Lucern yet, but everything was ready. Should she go knock on his bedroom door and risk making him grumpy? That would hardly aid her cause. Should she carry the breakfast up on a tray and give it to him in bed? That didn't seem like a good idea. After the dream she'd had last night, she thought it might be best to stay far away from Lucern and beds—otherwise she might jump the poor man in the hope that the real thing would be as good.

Sighing, Kate considered the table she had set, then glanced at the oven where she'd placed everything to keep it warm. The things would be all right there for a little bit, but not long. She decided she would just clean the mess she'd made in his kitchen, and if he wasn't up by the time she finished, she'd risk his temper to wake him up.

Spying a radio on the kitchen counter, she turned it on and set to work, boogying around the kitchen to a classic rock station.

It was a screechy death shriek from an animal that woke Lucern. At least, that was what he thought. He sat

116

up abruptly as the sound brought him awake, then paused to listen to the noises in his home.

Someone was banging around in the kitchen, and he could hear the tinny sound of music playing somewhere downstairs. But the shriek that had awakened him hadn't been either of these. Had it been Kate crying out in pain? he wondered, feeling himself tense. Was she being attacked by some madman who was even now destroying his kitchen?

"*Rahhhh-cksanne!*"

Lucern's eyes dilated in horror as the screechy voice sounded again, dragging along his nerves like nails on a chalkboard. Dear God, it was Kate attempting to sing.

He fell back with a grunt of disgust, exhaustion overwhelming him. He hadn't got to sleep until dawn. He was not ready to wake up yet.

"Roxanne!" the screech persisted.

It seemed *Kate* was ready for him to wake up, however.

Muttering under his breath, Lucern rose and stumbled into the shower. There he attempted to wake himself up and wash his bad mood away. He kept telling himself that he was getting rid of her today; he could sleep after that. It didn't help much. He was feeling incredibly grumpy as he staggered downstairs.

Kate heard Lucern on the steps and stopped singing. Whirling toward the stove, she grabbed pot holders, whipped the door open and quickly began retrieving breakfast. She was just setting the plate of hash browns on the table when he came into the kitchen.

"Good morning!" she sang cheerfully.

Lucern winced and groaned; then his gaze settled on

the table, and some of the grouchiness left his expression, replaced by surprise. "Did you make all this?"

"Yes," Kate breathed. She gave a sigh of relief. He wasn't going to be too terribly difficult about her waking him up. Just a *little* difficult. "Sit down and eat before it gets cold."

He sat and surveyed the offerings, then finally dug in. Kate poured coffee for them both, then joined him to eat. She allowed Lucern to eat in peace, deciding that she would broach the subject of doing an interview after he was full and happy.

Much to her surprise, however, she didn't end up having to.

When Lucern had finished his meal and pushed his plate away, Kate stood and grabbed the coffee pot to refill both their cups. She was working out what she would say as she set the pot back when Lucern suddenly said: "One event."

Kate turned back to the table in confusion. "One event?"

Lucern nodded. "If it's the only way to get rid of you, Kate C. Leever, I'll agree to one publicity thing."

"Really?" She tried to still the hope that leapt inside her. She waited for the catch.

"Yes. But this is the deal. I do the one event. One only. After that you have to let me alone."

"Okay," she agreed.

Lucern eyed her suspiciously. "You won't call and harass me anymore? No express letters? No camping on my doorstep?"

"No. I promise," Kate said solemnly.

"Very well." He sighed. "One event—preferably the R.T. thing my mother mentioned."

Kate's eyes nearly popped out of her head. "The R.T. thing?"

"Yes. Would my doing that keep your bosses happy?"

"Oh, yes," Kate breathed, hardly able to believe her luck. She'd mentioned the conference to Marguerite at the wedding, and admitted that she wished she could convince Lucern to attend, but she'd never guessed he would agree. It seemed the woman had taken up the cause. Kate decided she loved Marguerite Argeneau. Marguerite was a wonderful woman.

"Good. Then arrange it. I'll do the R.T. interview. Now, when are you going to leave me in peace?"

Kate glanced at the kitchen clock. It was almost noon. She had called earlier and found out there was a one-o'clock flight, a three-o'clock and a five-o'clock. She had thought she would have to take one of the later flights, and she still could if she wanted to spend more time with him. But then his words clicked. *"Good. Then I'll do the R.T. interview."* R.T. hadn't asked to do an interview yet. The only R.T. event was the conference. Had Lucern's mother led him astray? Deliberately?

"Er . . . Luc, what exactly did your mother say about the R.T. thing?"

Her author shrugged. "She said, 'I suggest you tell her you'll do R.T.' She thought it was probably the best option for both of us."

"And that's all she said?" Kate asked carefully.

Lucern nodded, then added, "Oh, and she said it was a magazine."

Kate had to consider this. Marguerite had led her son

119

astray all right, and the only reason she could imagine the other woman would do that was to try to help her. Kate felt a twinge of guilt.

A moment later, she let it go. Marguerite wouldn't do anything to harm her son. She must think he would go, too. And that it would be good for him. Kate wasn't going to get into the middle of it. He'd said he would do the R.T. "thing"; she would leave it at that.

She would also get the heck out of there before he realized it was a conference, not an interview, and tried to back out.

"Oh! I didn't realize it was so late," she gasped, peering at her wristwatch with feigned surprised. Then she smiled at Lucern sweetly. "You asked when I was going to leave you in peace. Well, there's a one-o'clock flight that I can just make if I hurry!"

And with that, she whirled and rushed out of the kitchen.

Lucern gaped at the swinging kitchen door. He'd wanted her gone, but her eagerness to comply was a bit disconcerting. He tilted his head and scowled at the ceiling as banging and bumping erupted upstairs. She was obviously rushing about like a crazywoman up there. It seemed she couldn't get out of his home fast enough. It also seemed she was mostly packed, because it wasn't long before he heard her rush along the hall overhead.

He stepped into the hall in time to see her rush down the stairs. A car honked out front at the same moment her foot landed on the ground floor.

"Oh!" Kate turned toward the kitchen, then paused. She smiled in relief when she saw him. "There you are!

120

Good! My taxi's here and I didn't want to leave without saying goodbye."

"Taxi?" Lucern echoed with disbelief.

"Yes. I called from my room while packing. Boy, they're fast here, huh?"

When Lucern simply stared at her blankly, Kate hesitated. Finally, hefting her suitcase she said, "Well. Thanks for everything. I know I was an unwanted guest, but you were pretty good about it, all things considered. And I appreciate—oh, damn!" she muttered as the cab honked again.

"Wait!" Lucern called as his editor turned and opened the front door. She hesitated, waving at the cab to let the driver know she was coming, then turned back. Lucern didn't really have anything to say; he was just reluctant to see her go. After searching his mind for something—anything—about which to speak, he finally came up with, "What about the interview? When will you arrange it? And you should have my phone number so that you can call and let me know when it is. And my e-mail address, too," he added as the thoughts struck him.

"Um . . ." She winced, then admitted, "Your mother gave me both your number and e-mail address."

"She did?" He was startled, though he knew he shouldn't be. Not with his busybody mother.

"Yes." Kate sidled a little further out the door, a fascinating expression on her face. She looked torn, as if she knew she had to tell him something but didn't really want to. Lucern's fascination deepened when she took another crablike step sideways before blurting, "R.T. doesn't want an interview."

"It doesn't?"

"No, they don't. The R.T. thing your mother was talking about is a *conference*." A look of pain crossed her face; then, while Lucern was trying to absorb that, she added, "But don't worry. You won't regret this. I'll be there with you and will look out for you the whole time." She was still sidling and had almost made it out the door as she added on a babble, "I'll send you all the information and the tickets and pick you up from the airport and everything. So don't worry!"

The taxi chose that moment to give another impatient honk.

"Gotta go!" Kate cried, and pulled the door closed with a slam. The sound echoed through the house, followed by the *tap-tap* of her rush down the porch steps. Then silence fell.

Lucern was transfixed. It was as if he had been pole-axed. Conference? His mother hadn't said anything about a conference. She'd said *Romantic Times* was a magazine. A book club. Someone who would want an interview. Kate must be confused. Dear God, she'd *better* be confused.

He hurried to the door and stared through the shaded glass just as the taxi pulled away. Lucern watched it.

He stood for a moment, Kate's words playing through his head; then he turned and started up the stairs. *R.T.* She must be confused. He would look up Romantic Times magazine on the Internet just to make sure she was confused.

Barely three minutes later, Lucern's roar echoed through the house.

Chapter Seven

"I am not doing it," Lucern announced, fury underlying his calm proclamation.

"Yes, you are." Marguerite Argeneau filled in another word in her daily crossword puzzle. She'd been working on the damned thing since he'd arrived.

Marguerite disliked the smell and noise of the city. Lucern's father, Claude, hadn't liked it any better. Besides which, living in the city meant moving every ten years to avoid drawing unwanted attention from the fact that they didn't age. Lucern's parents had avoided it all by purchasing several lots of land an hour outside of Toronto, and building their home in the midst of them. They thus had no neighbors near enough to be a concern, and needed not move at all if they did not wish. At least, they hadn't had to move in the thirty years since they'd built it.

Lucern now sat in the family mansion and watched his mother fill in another word. He had no idea why she bothered with the bloody crossword; centuries of living combined with a perfect memory made it less than challenging. Shrugging, he glared at her and repeated, "I am not doing it."

"You are."

"Am not."

"Are."

"Not."

"Are."

"All right, you two. Stop it," Bastien interrupted. He had ridden out to the Argeneau family home after Lucern had called him, ranting unintelligibly about being tricked and shouting that he was going to wring their precious mother's neck. Bastien hadn't really believed his brother would do it, but curiosity had made him rush out to see what would happen. He'd arrived just behind Lucern, entered the house on his brother's heels, and still didn't know what the man was upset about.

He really wanted to know. It was rare to see Lucern with the fire presently burning in his eyes. Grumpy, surly, impatient? Yes, Luc was often all of those. Impassioned with rage? No. Kate C. Leever had lit a fire under him the likes of which Bastien hadn't seen in his five hundred years. And Bastien *was* sure this had something to do with that inestimable editor. Luc had shouted her name like a curse several times while ranting on the phone. It was one of the few words Bastien had actually caught.

Turning to his brother, Bastien asked, "So what exactly is the problem, Luc? I thought you were willing to trade an interview with this *Romantic Weekly* magazine to get rid of Kate. What's happened to change that?"

"*Romantic Times*," Lucern corrected shortly. "And it isn't a bloody interview—that's what changed it. It's a damned conference."

"A conference?" Bastien glanced at his mother suspiciously. "Did you know this?"

Marguerite Argeneau shrugged mildly, which was as close as she would come to a confession. "I don't see the problem. It's just a couple days in a hotel with some readers."

"Five days, mother," Lucern snapped. "Five days in a hotel with some five thousand fans. And then there are balls, book-signings and—"

"One book-signing," his mother interrupted. "One book-signing with a couple hundred other writers there. You won't be the focus. You'll be lucky to get any attention at all."

Lucern was not calmed. "And what about the balls and awards dinners and—"

"All the functions are held in the hotel. You won't need to risk the sun. And—"

"I won't need to risk the sun because I'm not doing it!" Lucern roared. "I can't go."

"You *are* going," Marguerite began firmly, but Bastien interrupted her. "Why can't you go?" he asked Lucern.

"It's in the states, Bastien," his brother said grimly. "I can't possibly get blood through Customs at the airport. And I can't go without blood for five days." He could, actually, but not very comfortably. Cramps would cripple him, and his body would begin to consume itself.

Bastien frowned. "I could ship blood to you once you're there. We do such things all the time."

"There. You see!" Their mother crowed with triumph. "You are going."

"Thanks, Brother." Lucern sneered at the younger man, then glared ferociously at his mother. "I am *not* going!" he said again.

"You gave your word."

"I was tricked into giving my word. You led me to believe it was an interview."

"I never said it was an interview," Marguerite argued. Then she stressed, "You gave your word you would go and you are going."

"I may have given my word, but I didn't sign a contract or anything. I am not going."

Marguerite jerked upright as if he had slapped her. Her words were slow and cold. "A man's word used to be his bond."

Lucern flinched, but he growled, "It used to be. Times have changed. In this world, a man doesn't have to do anything unless it is in writing."

"In this day and age, that's true," she allowed, eyes narrowing on him. "But that isn't how you were raised, Lucern Argeneau. Are you no longer a man of your word?"

Luc gritted his teeth, his fury and helplessness combining. His mother was pulling out the big guns, questioning his honor and using his full name to show her shame that he would even suggest going back on his word. Could he really disappoint her?

Kate chewed on her thumbnail and paced the carpet by the arrivals gate. Her plane had arrived early and Lucern Argeneau's plane was late, which meant she'd been waiting for nearly two hours. And she wasn't even sure if Lucern was on the plane.

She had sent the tickets and all the information on the Romantic Times Conference the day after leaving Toronto. She hadn't received a letter back stating that Lucern would *not* be coming, but then neither had she received word that he would. For all Kate knew, he hadn't even read her damned letter. As usual. She could have called—she had the number—but Kate suddenly found she had a yellow streak. She hadn't called for fear that he would tell her where she could stick her tickets.

Groaning, she turned and paced back the way she'd come. It had been four weeks and three days since she'd left Toronto. She had been petted and congratulated that entire time in the offices of Roundhouse Publishing. Allison had been amazed that she had succeeded where Edwin had failed—a nice little tidbit they had neglected to mention. It seemed her job hadn't been in jeopardy after all; but her convincing Lucern to attend the conference had raised her in their esteem. Allison was now positive that Kate "could get the job done." Her position was secure.

Barring any big screw-up on her part, she added to herself. Which would include Lucern's simply not showing up after all the money they had put into registering him, purchasing his first-class plane tickets, and securing the three-room suite she'd insisted on getting at the hotel. Kate had told Allison she'd promised Lucern these arrangements. And in a way she had; she'd promised him on the way out the door that she would be sure he didn't regret coming, and that she'd be with

127

him at all times to ensure everything went well.

She'd considered how best to make him happy on the flight back to New York, and she'd continued to plan at home that night, thinking that if she got to the office on Monday to find a message from Lucern refusing to attend, she could pull all these special arrangements out to try to persuade him. It turned out she hadn't needed to persuade him, but she would still follow through on all the things she'd planned.

She would be glued to Lucern's side almost twenty-four hours a day, and when she couldn't be there—for instance, when he had to use the men's washroom, or when she had to slip away to the women's—someone else would be there. She had enlisted Chris Keyes, one of the two male editors at Roundhouse Publishing, to aid her in the endeavor.

She'd been prepared to beg, bribe and even resort to blackmail to get the senior editor to assist her, but in the end, she hadn't had to do any of that. Despite the fact that Chris had a slew of his own writers to look after at the conference, he had immediately agreed to help her.

Kate supposed the promise of his own room in a three-room suite, rather than sharing a normal two-bed room with Tom, the V.P. of Promotion, had helped. But C.K., as she sometimes called him, was also a big fan of Lucern's vampire series. Chris had asked a ton of questions about the man after Kate's return from Toronto, but she had just kept answering with, "You'll be meeting him soon. Wait and see." She'd been terrified that if she told him the truth, he'd refuse to help.

An increase in the noise level around her drew Kate's

attention to a mass of people moving up the hall. The plane had arrived, and she was about to find out if Lucern had come. Kate prayed his mother had badgered him into it, but she wasn't at all sure even that formidable woman could manage to do so.

Hands fisted at her sides, Kate searched the crowd of approaching faces. The conference officially began on Wednesday; but she had booked Lucern on a Tuesday-evening flight to prevent his using his allergy to sunlight as an excuse not to come. She and Chris had flown in early to meet him. Their arrivals had been an hour apart, precluding Kate from risking going to the hotel and checking in and then returning to collect Lucern, so Chris had good-naturedly taken control of their baggage and headed to the hotel while Kate waited for Lucern's flight.

Mind you, had she realized that Lucern's flight was going to be delayed so long, she might have gone with Chris and stopped for a drink or two or three before returning. She was so nervous about this conference that she was developing a sour stomach. Or perhaps it was an ulcer—she had heard that was a common editors' complaint.

Kate's thoughts died abruptly as her gaze settled on a man who had been somewhere near the back of the pack. She'd recognize anywhere that muscular frame and the majestic way he held his head. *Lucern*. He was bearing down on her, his long-legged stride quickly bringing him to the front of the disembarking passengers.

"Thank you, Marguerite," she whispered, not even caring that the man looked as surly as ever. She would expect nothing less. He was here, and that was all that mattered. A smile of relief stretching her lips, Kate moved forward to greet him.

"You came." She hadn't intended to speak those words, or for her relief to show, but so it was.

Lucern scowled. "I said I would. I'm a man of my word."

Kate's smile widened even further; then she glanced down at the suitcase, overnight bag, briefcase and portable computer he held. "Here, let me take those for you."

She relieved him of the briefcase and portable computer before he could stop her. He didn't appear pleased by her help.

"I can carry my own things, thank you," he said. His words were stiff, and he tried to retrieve the articles. Kate ignored the attempt and merely turned to lead the way out, babbling with determined cheer. "Chris went ahead to the hotel to check us in, so all we have to do is ride there and settle in. I arranged for your flight to be tonight because I recalled you were allergic to the sun. The best I could do was to have you leave late in the afternoon and arrive in the early evening, which I figured was better than leaving and arriving in the daytime. This works out nicely, though, because now we have the whole night to relax before the others show up tomorrow."

Lucern had been scowling at Kate's back—her heart-shaped butt, actually, if he was honest—but at those words he jerked his eyes up to the back of her head and grimaced. He had wondered why his flight was booked for the night before the conference began, but he had just supposed it was what everyone did. Now he knew she'd done it out of concern for him. Or, more likely, concern that he would refuse to fly during day-light due to his "allergy." What a pain; now he had to be grateful.

"Here we are."

Lucern had been debating commenting on her kind-ness in having him fly at night, but gave up the idea as he saw the car she'd stopped beside. It was a black sedan, mini limo. She handed his portable and brief-case to the driver with a smile, then turned and tried to take Lucern's overnight bag while waiting for the driver to stow the items in the trunk. Lucern frowned and evaded her reaching hands. He moved to the trunk and put them in himself. The silly woman was trying to be helpful, but Lucern was used to things being the other way around. In the era in which he'd been raised and his attitudes formed, *he* was supposed to carry things for *her*—not allow her to carry his burden.

The driver closed the trunk and led the way to the back passenger door where Kate stood. Apparently, she didn't appreciate Lucern's gallantry in refusing her help. That fact was just as exasperating to Lucern. Someone should teach the silly woman that men were given the physical strength to bear the burdens in life. Women were given beauty to please the men. Deciding to ignore her, he followed her into the back seat when the driver opened the door, then fixed a dignified you-don't-exist-for-me look on his face and stared straight ahead.

The moment the door closed, he was enveloped in a cloud of her tantalizing perfume. He didn't know

131

what it was she wore, but it should come with a warning: "Heady, and likely to cause confusion in those who smell it." He himself was certainly suffering confusion from it.

Annoyance overtook him. He'd been feeling betrayed for four weeks, ever since she'd rushed out of his house, and he'd been nursing that anger. Yet now, as the smell of Kate's perfume surrounded him, his anger was overwhelmed by an entirely different but equally passionate reaction.

Men suffered a terrible handicap, he decided with disgust as he found his anger edged out by lust. The amazing thing was that it had taken him six hundred years to recognize that fact.

"I tried to do everything I could to make sure this was as comfortable for you as possible," Kate said, drawing his attention. "What I'd like to do is outline what I've arranged. Then, if you have any suggestions, perhaps I could take care of them tonight so we'll be all ready before everyone else arrives. Okay?"

Lucern grunted assent, then wished he hadn't when she dug out a file from her capacious purse and shifted closer so that he could watch her open it. He really didn't want her closer. The scent of her was upsetting enough to his equilibrium; the feel of her was going to be . . .

Lucern inhaled deeply and sighed as she opened the file and unintentionally brushed his arm with hers. Then his gaze landed on the top page of the agenda. He frowned. "According to this, the conference started on Sunday."

"No," Kate said. Then she corrected herself, "Well,

yes. They had some events for anyone who wanted to join ahead of time, but the official start isn't until tomorrow."

"Hmm." Lucern decided to keep his mouth shut. He should be grateful that she hadn't forced him to go through the pre-conference crap, too.

"So," his editor said with a return of her determined cheer. "Tomorrow starts with the morning walk with cover models. Then the brunch—"

"What the deuce is a morning walk with cover models?" Lucern interrupted. He'd already seen the agenda, of course—both on the internet and in the paperwork she'd sent him. But nothing had described any of the listed events.

"Er . . . well, actually, I'm not sure," she admitted. She cleared her throat, her smile a tad strained. "But it doesn't matter—you don't have to attend."

"I don't?" He peered at her suspiciously. Something she didn't want him to attend? That seemed strange. He had been sure that she was going to drag him to every single function.

"No. Your first official event will be the Welcome Brunch and R.T. Awards."

Lucern nodded. Those didn't sound so bad. He could eat. Although the awards part would probably be boring.

"Then there's the Reader Hospitality Suite and discussion," she went on. "Allison and Chuck want you there."

"Who are Allison and Chuck?"

"Allison is the head editor, my boss," Kate explained. "And Chuck is the company president. They'll definitely

133

expect you to attend the Hospitality Suite."

Lucern grimaced. "What is it?"

"It's . . ." She appeared to be at a loss for a moment. "Well, each publisher—most of them, anyway—rents out a reception room at the hotel, and writers and editors talk to the readers who come in."

"You want me to talk to people?" he asked in horror. Dear God, he should have done the signing! That would have been less bother, just scribbling his name.

"Of course I want you to talk to people," Kate said with exasperation. "You can do it. I've seen you speak." She fell silent and stared at him, alarm growing on her face. She bit her lip. "Or maybe we can skip that. No, Allison and Chuck would have a fit. You have to go." She sighed heavily. "Oh, damn. This isn't good."

"No, it isn't," Lucern agreed with a nod. Then he jerked around with surprise as the door opened beside him. They had apparently arrived. Without his realizing it, the car had stopped, and the driver was now waiting for him to alight. Nodding his thanks, Lucern slid out then turned and took Kate's hand when she followed.

"We'll need to work on you tonight," she decided as she straightened next to him.

Lucern stiffened and dropped her hand. "Work on me?"

"Yes. Work on you," Kate repeated. They followed Lucern's luggage into the hotel. It was on a trolley, being pulled by a uniformed bellhop. Apparently the driver had seen to the luggage before opening the door for them.

"I don't need 'work,' " Lucern said irritably as they stopped at the elevator.

"Yes, Lucern, you do." Kate smiled sweetly at the bell-hop as the doors opened, and he gestured for them to enter.

"I do not," Lucern insisted, following, squeezing himself up against Kate to leave room for the luggage trolley.

"Can we talk about this later?"

Kate gave an impatient nod at the bellhop and pushed the button for their floor. At least Lucern presumed it was their floor. He hadn't a clue, though she had said someone named Chris had already checked them in. He supposed this Chris was another editor. He wondered if she would be as annoying as Kate.

He glanced at the bellhop, confused at Kate's desire to put this off. The man was a servant, hardly worth worrying about. Although he didn't want to argue either. "No. There is nothing to discuss. I do not need to be worked on."

"You do," Kate insisted. "And I'm not going to talk about this now."

"There is nothing to talk about."

"There *is*," she snapped.

The bellhop gave a soft chuckle, and Lucern glared at him. There had been a time when servants knew their place and would have been deaf and dumb to such discussions. That time wasn't now. He constantly forgot how rude the world had become.

The doors opened and the bellhop moved the trolley out; then he led them down a long hall past countless doors. At the end he stopped, pulled out a card key, opened the door, then pushed the trolley in.

"Which room do these go in, ma'am?" he asked,

pausing in the center of a large chamber set up as a living room.

His question drew another scowl from Lucern. He was the man; the fellow should have addressed the question to him.

"I'm not sure. Just set them here. We can manage, thanks." Kate accepted the card key from the fellow and handed him a tip, making Lucern scowl again, this time at himself. He was the man; he should have tipped the bellhop. He should be more on the ball. His only excuse was that it had been a long day. His flight had been at three p.m., but he'd had to leave for the airport at one to get through security. He had worn a business suit, hat and sunglasses, and slathered on sunscreen, but of course, some of the sunlight had got through. His body had sustained damage that his blood was already working to correct. He was feeling depleted and needed to feed—a state he was beginning to associate with Kate Leever.

The click of the door closing drew his gaze back to her, and Lucern picked up their argument immediately. "I do not need to be worked on."

"Lucern," his editor began wearily. Suddenly losing her temper, she said grimly, "Look. You're named after a dairy product, you look like an Angel wannabe, and you talk like a bad Bela Lugosi. You need work!"

"Wow, Kate."

Lucern turned to see a tall, slender blond man entering the room. He was clapping his hands slowly, an irrepressible grin on his face. "You'll have to give me pointers on handling writers. I've never seen it done quite like that."

"Oh. Chris." Kate sighed unhappily.

"This is Chris?" Lucern asked with dismay.

His editor stiffened again but said simply, "Yes."

"You never said he was a man. Make him leave."

Kate's eyes narrowed on him, fury burning out of them. "Look, Lucern—"

"Nope," Chris interjected. He put his hands up in a conciliatory gesture. "Kate, he doesn't sound like Bela Lugosi. The smarmy accent is missing."

Kate's ire turned on her coworker. "I meant he uses old-fashioned terminology."

Chris merely arched an eyebrow. A moment later he added, "And his hair's too dark for him to be an Angel wannabe."

"Shut up! Stay out of this."

The editor laughed, apparently unoffended. "And Allison and Chuck were worried you couldn't handle this guy."

"Who *is* this gentleman?" Lucern asked Kate stiffly. If she said it was her husband, boyfriend or lover, he feared he might have to perform some violence.

"Chris Keyes," Kate announced. "He's an editor at Roundhouse, too. Chris Keyes, meet Lucern Argeneau, aka Luke Amirault, the vampire writer."

"A pleasure, Mr. Argeneau." The lanky editor stepped forward and offered his hand in welcome.

Lucern automatically shook, but he asked, "You're an editor?"

Keyes nodded.

"What do you edit?"

"Romance, like Kate."

Lucern nodded slowly, then asked hopefully, "Are you a homosexual?"

Chris Keyes's eyes rounded in shock.

"Lucern!"

Lucern glanced at Kate with annoyance. She sounded just like his mother when she barked like that. Taking in the way his editor was flushing and then paling by turns, he decided not to mention it.

A sudden burst of laughter drew his gaze back to Chris. The young man's stunned expression had given way to a deep belly laugh. Lucern waited patiently for him to recover himself.

When Chris's mirth had died down to a chuckle, he asked, "What made you ask such a question?"

"You are a romance editor. That is a woman's job."

"Ah." Chris grinned. "But you write them. Are you gay?"

Lucern stared for a moment, then grinned, caught. "Touché."

Kate was not amused. Moving between the two, she glared up at Lucern. "Chris has kindly agreed to help look after you this weekend. You will not be rude to him." She scowled and added, "At least, no ruder than you usually are."

Lucern scowled back. "I do not need to be looked after."

"You—"

"Kate," Chris interrupted. "It's getting late. If you still want to go to Bobbi's kick-off party, you should probably—"

"Oh, damn!" Kate glanced at her watch. She seemed to forget all about Lucern and asked her coworker,

138

"Where did you put my stuff? It's a Western theme. I have to change."

"I put it in that room." Chris pointed to a door on their right. "I figured if you didn't like it, we could shuffle later."

Kate merely nodded. Rushing into the room, she slammed the door behind her. Chris just shook his head.

Lucern scowled after Kate. If she expected him to go to this party, she had another think coming. He had no intention of going to a Western themed party after just flying in.

"So, I guess it's you and me tonight, Luc," Chris said cheerfully. Lucern suddenly rethought the party. Kate would be there. Not this guy.

"Why are you here?" he asked the male editor.

Chris grinned. "I'm supposed to keep you safe. When Kate can't be around. Like tonight."

"Keep me safe?" Lucern echoed. "From what?"

Chris pursed his lips and considered. Then he grinned. "You've never been to a Romantic Times conference, have you, Luc?"

Lucern shook his head. He gave a start of surprise when Chris clapped a hand on his shoulder and steered him toward the bar in the corner. "Let's have a drink while I tell you. You're going to need it."

Lucern fretted as he watched Chris pour the glass of Scotch he requested. He was beginning to believe this conference would be even more of a pain than he'd feared.

"There you are." Chris handed him his drink. The editor then gestured for them to move to the couch, which was set against the walled window.

Lucern moved toward it, suddenly thinking how hungry he was. "Was there a package delivered here for me?"

"Not that I know of. I'm sure they would have mentioned it when I signed in," Chris answered. He settled in the room's one chair, leaving the couch to Lucern. "But then, I don't know that your name is registered for this room."

Lucern stiffened. Was he not to be the man in any of these situations?

The bedroom door Kate had disappeared through suddenly opened, and she rushed out. Lucern automatically got to his feet at her entrance, forgetting about his hoped for blood delivery. He gaped at the woman. She was wearing the tightest pair of hip-hugging jeans he had seen in all his born days. They were complemented by knee-high cowboy boots, a checkered shirt, a fringed suede jacket, and a cowboy hat that looked like it had seen rough use. She looked sexy as hell.

"Katie," Chris called. "Did you put Lucern's name on the room?"

Kate glanced over with surprise. "Of course not. I was afraid someone might connect the names Lucern Argeneau and Lucern Argentus and figure out this was his room. The whole idea of this suite was so that none of his fans could find him. Why?"

"Luc was expecting a delivery. I guess they would have turned it away if they didn't think he was here."

Kate turned an apologetic gaze on Lucern. "Sorry. Just call and have them deliver it to my name. Okay?"

Lucern nodded slowly, his eyes feasting on her. She

blushed under his perusal, then said, "I'll try not to be out late. Chris will look after you until I get back. Anything you want, he's the man to go to, okay?"

Lucern nodded again, his tongue stuck on the roof of his mouth.

"Chris." She turned her attention to her coworker. "Make him watch some TV. Maybe he can update the way he speaks by watching it."

The other editor laughed. "Katie, dear, if watching television hasn't changed his speech before now, one night is hardly going to do it."

"He doesn't have a TV," she explained dryly. "At least, I didn't see one." She turned a curious gaze to Lucern. "*Do* you have one?"

He shook his head. Television, in his opinion, rotted the brain.

"I didn't think so," she said with satisfaction. She instructed her friend "Make him watch it. I'll see you guys later."

Both men were silent until the door closed behind Kate. Lucern sank back onto the couch.

"Why did you stand?" Chris asked curiously.

"A lady had entered the room," Lucern answered absently. His vision was still full of Kate the cowgirl. He usually preferred women in more feminine dress, but there had been nothing masculine about Kate in that outfit.

"You're kidding about the TV, right?" Chris asked. "Do you really not have one?"

"No. Never have."

"Man!" Chris picked up the remote control off the table. Lucern recognized it; he had one for his stereo system at home. This was to the television. The editor clicked it and grinned. "You're in for a treat, Luc. You're gonna love television."

Lucern grimaced. He very much doubted that he would love television. He was more a theater type of guy. Old habits died hard.

Chapter Eight

Lucern loved television. He didn't know why he had allowed prejudice to prevent him from at least trying it before now. TV was a marvelous invention. It was like a mini-stage with little players. And what players! In the last three hours he had watched a movie by some guy named Monty Python . . . or had that been the character?

Anyway, they'd watched that first. When it ended, Chris had looked through a television guide and cried, "Yeah! A Black Adder marathon!" And they'd been watching that ever since. It was a grand show! Marvelous and amusing. Lucern hadn't laughed so hard in years.

"They have history all mixed up, but it is quite amusing," he announced, reaching for a fresh beer from the six-pack on the coffee table.

Chris burst out laughing, then stopped abruptly, his eyes going wide. "Oh, shoot! Kate's going to kill me!"

Lucern arched his eyebrows. "Why?"

"Because I was supposed to make you watch modern American television, to help with your speech." He pondered for a minute before shrugging. "What the hell. It's kind of late in the game to change your speech, anyway."

Lucern nodded absently. The mention of Kate made him remember her accusations of earlier. She had said he spoke in old-fashioned ways. Lucern supposed he did; it was hard to change speech patterns. He'd been born in Switzerland in 1390. His parents had moved around a lot in those days, but that was where he'd been conceived and born. They had subsequently moved back to England, and he had learned to speak using the King's English. Despite all the countries he had lived in since, and all the languages he had learned and spoken, he still did and probably always would bear a slight accent and lean toward speaking the way he'd been taught.

What else had she said? He recalled something about an angel. That he looked like an angel wannabe? What did that mean exactly? Her voice had been too snarly for it to be a compliment. His gaze shifted from the TV screen to Chris. "Who, or what, is an angel wannabe?"

Chris turned a blank expression on him. "Huh?"

"Kate said I looked like an angel wannabe," Lucern reminded him. Understanding immediately lit the young editor's face. "Oh, yeah. Well, you know. Angel. Buffy and Angel? Vampire slayer and vamp? Oh, that's right. You don't watch TV, so you wouldn't know," he said finally. "Well, Angel is this vampire, see. And he is,

little miss Tiny

by Roger Hargreaves

WORLD INTERNATIONAL
MANCHESTER

Little Miss Tiny was extremely small.

Not very tall at all!

She was so very tiny she didn't live in a house.

Do you know where she lived?

In a mousehole, in the dining room of
Home Farm.

She had made the mousehole quite comfortable really, and luckily there weren't any mice because the farm cat had chased them all away.

The trouble was, because she was so tiny, nobody knew she lived there.

Nobody had noticed her.

Not even the farmer and his wife.

So, there she lived.

All alone.

With nobody to talk to.

She was very lonely.

And sad.

Oh dear!

One day she was feeling so lonely she decided to be very brave and go for a walk.

Out of her mousehole she came.

She crept across the dining room and went through the crack in the door and into the hall.

To little Miss Tiny the hall looked as big as a field, and she scuttled across it to the back door of the farm.

Luckily for her the letterbox was at the bottom of the door and she squeezed herself through it and onto the doorstep.

It was all very exciting!

There before her was the farmyard.

She went exploring.

She came to a door with a gap at the bottom, and ducked in underneath.

There, inside, was a pig.

A large pig!

And, if you're as small as little Miss Tiny, a large pig looks very large indeed.

Miss Tiny looked at the pig.

The pig looked at Miss Tiny.

"Oink," he grunted, and moved closer to inspect this little person who had entered his sty.

"Oh my goodness me," squeaked little Miss Tiny in alarm, and shot out of the pigsty as fast as ever her little legs would carry her.

Which wasn't very fast because her legs were so very little!

She ran right around to the back of the pigsty before she stopped.

She leaned against the wall and put her hands over her eyes, and tried to get her breath back.

Suddenly, she heard a noise.

A very close noise.

A sort of breathing noise.

Very close indeed!

Oh!

She hardly dared take her hands away from her eyes, but when she did she wished she hadn't.

What do you think it was, there, right in front of her, looking at her with green eyes?

Ginger!

The farm cat!!

Poor little Miss Tiny.

Ginger grinned, showing his teeth.

"HELP!" shrieked Miss Tiny at the top of
her voice.

"Oh somebody please HELP!"

The trouble was, the top of little Miss Tiny's
voice was not a very loud place.

Ginger grinned another grin.

Every day Mr Strong went to Home Farm
to buy some eggs.

He liked eggs.

Lots of them.

That day he was walking home across the
farmyard when he heard a very tiny squeak.

He stopped.

There it was again.

Round the corner.

He looked round the corner and saw Ginger
and the poor trapped little Miss Tiny.

"SHOO!" said Mr Strong to Ginger, and picked up little Miss Tiny.

Very gently.

"Hello," he said. "Who are you?"

"I'm... I'm... I'm... Miss Tiny."

"You are, aren't you?" smiled Mr Strong.

"Well, if I was as tiny as you, I wouldn't go wandering around large farmyards!"

"But..." said Miss Tiny, and told Mr Strong about how she was so lonely she had to come out to find somebody to talk to.

"Oh dear," said Mr Strong. "Well now, let's see if we can't find you some friends to talk to."

And now, every week, Mr Strong collects little Miss Tiny and takes her off to see her friends.

Three weeks ago he took her to see Mr Funny, who told her so many jokes she just couldn't stop laughing all day.

Two weeks ago he took her to see Mr Greedy.

He told her his recipe for his favourite meal.

"But that's much much too much for tiny little me," she laughed.

Mr Greedy grinned.

"For you," he said, "divide by a hundred!"

Last week Mr Strong took her to see Mr Silly.

And Mr Silly showed her how to stand on your head.

"That's very silly," giggled little Miss Tiny.

"Thank you," replied Mr Silly, modestly.

And guess who she met this week?

Somebody who's become a special little friend.

"I never thought I'd ever meet anybody smaller than myself," laughed Mr Small.

Little Miss Tiny looked up at him, and smiled.

"You wait till I grow up", she said.